Peter smiled. "I'd rather talk about you."

"And I would rather go to bed."

No sooner had Bethany uttered the words than her cheeks turned an electrifying shade of pink. "I mean my bed. Alone. To sleep," she added with an almost desperate note in her voice.

Peter let her off the hook. "Relax, Bethany. I didn't take that to be an invitation."

She was relieved, and yet...not so relieved. "Why not?" she demanded. "Do you find me unattractive?"

He looked at her. "If anyone could pull me out of my workaholic state, it would be you." He paused, adding, "As long as you promised not to launch into another debate in the middle of a heated embrace."

Flustered and pleased, Bethany was at a loss for words. She didn't want to encourage him.

Yet if she were being totally honest with herself, she didn't want to completely *dis*courage him, either.

Dear Reader,

Welcome to the first book of the Wilder saga, featuring two brothers, two sisters and a hospital. We first meet the siblings at a sad occasion, the funeral of their father, Dr. James Wilder, a man much loved by the community. James was an old-fashioned kind of doctor, and "his" hospital, Walnut River General, has attracted a handful of excellent doctors, two of whom are Peter Wilder and his younger sister, Ella.

This is Peter's book. The forty-year-old internist is a carbon copy of his father, and with his father's passing, he finds himself suddenly filling shoes he feels can never be filled. He also finds himself in the middle of a battle. A major conglomerate is trying to initiate a hospital takeover, and size and money are on its side. The conglomerate also has Bethany Holloway, the newest member of the hospital's board of directors, a smart, driven woman who thinks Peter is standing in the way of progress and the future. Battle lines are drawn, then blurred as each finds themselves also involved in a war of emotions, because the immovable object and the irresistible force are *very* drawn to one another.

I hope you enjoy this story and come back for more. And, as ever, I thank you for reading and wish you someone to love who loves you back.

Marie Ferrarella

MARIE FERRARELLA

FALLING FOR THE M.D.

SPECIAL EDITION®

Published by Silhouette Books

America's Publisher of Contemporary Romance

Special thanks and acknowledgment are given
to Marie Ferrarella for her contribution to
THE WILDER FAMILY miniseries.

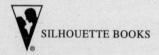 SILHOUETTE BOOKS

ISBN-13: 978-0-373-28121-3
ISBN-10:   0-373-28121-8

FALLING FOR THE M.D.

Books by Marie Ferrarella

MARIE FERRARELLA

This *USA TODAY* bestselling and RITA® Award-winning author has written more than one hundred and fifty novels for Harlequin and Silhouette Books, some under the name Marie Nicole. Her romances are beloved by fans worldwide.

To
Gail Chasan
And the Joy of
Family Sagas

Chapter One

He'd known this day was coming for a long time.

Death was not a surprise to him. As a doctor, it was all part of the circle of life. But while he always concentrated on the positive, Dr. Peter Wilder could never fully ignore the fact that death was seated at the very same table as life.

His mother, Alice, had died five years ago, a victim of cancer. Now that death had come to rob him for a second time, though, he felt alone, despite the fact that the cemetery was crowded. His three siblings were there, along with all the friends and admirers that his father, Dr. James Wilder, had garnered over the years as a physician and Chief of Staff at Walnut River General Hospital and, toward the end, as the chairman of the board of directors. Despite the cold, gloomy January morning and the persistent snow flurries, there had been an enormous turnout to pay last respects to a man who had touched so very many lives.

Despite all of his professional obligations, James had never failed to make time for his family, was always there for all the important occasions that meant something to his sons and daughters.

Now both his mother and his father were gone, the latter leaving behind incredibly large shoes to fill.

Peter had become the patriarch. As the oldest, he would be the one to whom David and Ella and Anna would turn.

Well, maybe not Anna, he reconsidered, glancing over toward her.

They were gathered around the grave. Typically, while he, David and Ella were on one side of his father's final resting place, Anna had positioned herself opposite them. Ten years his junior, Anna was the family's official black sheep.

While he, David and Ella had followed their father's footsteps, Anna's feet had not quite fit the mold. He knew that she had tried, managing to go so far as being accepted into a medical school. But then she'd dropped out in her freshman year.

Anna didn't have the head for medicine, or the heart. So she had gone a different route, earning an MBA and finally finding herself when she entered the world of finance.

But there was an even greater reason why the rest of them considered Anna to be the black sheep. His father had been fond of referring to her as "the chosen one," but the simple truth of it was, Anna had been a foundling, abandoned as an

infant on the steps of the hospital to which
the senior Wilder had dedicated his entire
adult life.

Since James Wilder lived and breathed
all things that concerned Walnut River
General, it somehow seemed natural that
he should adopt the only baby who had
ever been left there.

Or so he'd heard his father say to his
mother when he was trying to win her over
to his decision. His mother tried, but he
knew that she could never quite make
herself open her heart to this child whose
own parents hadn't wanted her. Maybe
because of this, because of the way his
mother felt, his father had done his best to
make it up to Anna. He had overcompensated.

For years, James went out of his way to
make Anna feel accepted and a wanted
member of the family. In his efforts to
keep Anna from feeling unloved, James
Wilder often placed his adopted daughter
first.

Despite all his good intentions, his

father's actions were not without conse-
quences. While they were growing up,
Peter and his siblings were resentful of the
special treatment Anna received. Especially David, who began to act out in order
to win his own brand of attention from
their father.

Slowly, so slowly that Peter wasn't even
certain when it actually happened, it
became a matter of their breaking into two
separate camps—he, David and Ella on
the one hand, and Anna, by herself, on the
other. The schism continued to grow
despite all of their father's efforts to the
contrary. Time and again, James would
try to rectify the situation, asking them
each what was wrong and what he could
do to fix it, only to be told by a tight-lipped
child that everything was fine.

But it wasn't.

He, David and Ella felt that Anna had
their father's ear and the bulk of his love
and attention. At the same time Anna, he
surmised as he looked back on things now,
probably felt like the odd woman out,

doomed to remain on the outside of the family circle, forever looking in.

Maybe now would be a good time to put a stop to it, Peter thought. To change direction and start fresh. As a tribute to his father, who simply wanted his family to all get along. They weren't all that different, really, the four of them. And Anna had loved James Wilder as much as any of them.

Snow was dusting Peter's dark brown hair, making it appear almost white. He brushed some of it aside. The sudden movement had Ella looking up at him. Ella, with her doelike eyes and small mouth that was usually so quick to smile shyly. Ella, whose dark eyes right now looked almost haunted with sadness.

Leaning her head toward him, she whispered, "I can't believe he's really gone. I thought he'd be with us forever, like some force of nature."

Standing on her other side, David couldn't help overhearing. "Well, he really is gone. They're about to lower the coffin," he murmured bitterly.

Ella's head jerked up and she looked at David, stunned at the raw pain in his tone, not just over the loss of their father, but the opportunity to ever again make things right between them. James and David had not been on the warmest terms at the time of the senior Wilder's death and Peter was certain that David chafed over words he had left unsaid simply because "there was always tomorrow."

Now tomorrow would never come.

Peter turned away, his attention on the highly polished casket slowly being lowered into the ground. With each inch that came between them, he felt fresh waves of loss wash over him.

Goodbye, Dad. I wish we'd had more time together. There's so much I still need to know, so much I still want to ask you.

Peter waited until the coffin was finally placed at the bottom of the grave, then he stepped forward and dropped the single red rose he'd been holding. It fell against the coffin and then, like the tears of a weeping mourner, slid off to the side.

"Rest well, Dad," Peter said, struggling to keep his voice from cracking. "You've earned it." And then he moved aside, letting Ella have her moment as she added her rose to his, her wishes to his.

One by one, the mourners all filed by, people who were close to the man, people who worshipped the doctor, dropping roses and offering warm words for one of the finest men any of them had ever known.

Peter had expected Anna to follow either David or, more likely since she'd once been close to her, Ella. But she stood off to the side, patiently waiting for everyone else to go by before she finally moved forward herself.

He should have realized that she wanted to be alone with their father one last time.

Last but not least, right, Anna?

She was saying something, but her voice was so low when she spoke that he couldn't hear her. He caught a glimpse of the tears glistening in her eyes even though she tried to avert her head so her grief would remain as private as her parting words.

Peter felt a hint of guilt pricking his conscience. This was his sister. Adopted, yes, but raised with him from infancy. She'd been only a few days old at most when his father had brought her into their house.

"I brought you an early birthday present, Alice," the senior Wilder had announced as he came through the front door.

Until the day he died, Peter would remember the look of surprise, disbelief and then something more that he couldn't begin to fathom wash across his mother's face when she came into the living room to see what it was that his father had brought home for her. He was ten at the time and David was six. His mother had just crawled out of a depression that had her, for a time, all but confined to her bed. He remembered how afraid he'd been back then, afraid that there was something wrong with his mother. He'd fully expected her to fall head over heels in love with the baby—that's what women did, he'd thought at the time. They loved babies.

But there had been a tightness around her mouth as she took the bundle from his father.

"She's very pretty, isn't she, boys?" his father had said, trying to encourage them to become part of the acceptance process.

"She's noisy," David had declared, scowling. "And she smells."

His father had laughed. "She just needs changing."

"Can we change her for a pony?" David wanted to know, picking up on the word.

"'Fraid not, David. What do you think of her, Peter?" his father had asked, turning toward him.

"She's very little" had been his only comment about this new addition. He remembered watching his mother instead of the baby. Watching and worrying. His father had once said that he was born old, and there was some truth to that. He couldn't remember ever being carefree.

"That's right," his father had agreed warmly. "And we need to look out for her." His father had placed his large, capable hand on his shoulder, silently conveying that he was counting on him. "You need to look after her. You're her big brother."

He remembered nodding solemnly, not happy about the assignment but not wanting to disappoint his father, either. He also recalled seeing his mother frown as she took the baby from his father and walked into the other room.

And so began a rather unsteady, continuing family dynamic. David saw Anna as competition, while Peter regarded Anna as a burden he was going to have to carry. And things never really changed.

For one reason or another, things were never quite harmonious among them. Whenever he would extend the olive branch, Anna would hold him suspect. And whenever she would seek common ground with him, he'd be too busy to meet her halfway. Things between her and

David were in an even worse state. Only she and Ella got along.

And so the years melted away, wrapped in misunderstanding and hurt feelings, and the gap continued to widen.

It was time to put a stop to it.

"Anna," he called to her.

David and Ella, standing nearby, both turned to look at their older brother. About to melt back into the crowd, Anna looked up and in Peter's direction. The wind whipped her light blond hair into her eyes. She blinked, pushing the strand back behind her ear, a silent question in her pale blue eyes.

Peter cut the distance between them. He couldn't shake the feeling that he was on borrowed time, that there was a finite amount of it during which he could bring peace to the family. He had no idea where the feeling had come from.

However, once he was beside her, words seemed to desert him. Ordinarily, he always knew how to sympathize, how to comfort. His bedside manner was one of his strongest points. He had absolutely no trouble placing himself in his patient's drafty hospital gown, understanding exactly what he or she was going through. Like his father before him, Peter's capacity for empathy was enormous, and his patients loved him for it.

But this was different. This was almost too personal. This came with baggage and history. His and Anna's.

Peter did his best to sound warm when he spoke to her, knowing that she had to be feeling the same sort of pain he was.

"There's going to be a reception at my house." David and Ella were standing directly behind him. He wished one of them would say something. "I didn't know if you knew." Once the words were out, he realized it sounded like a backhanded invitation.

"I didn't," she replied quietly. Her eyes moved from David's face to Ella's to his again.

She looked as if she wanted to leave, Peter thought. He couldn't really blame her.

He knew there'd be less tension if she did. But then again, it wasn't right to drive her away.

Peter tried again. "I thought it might help everyone to get together, swap a few stories about Dad. Everyone seems to have a hundred of them," he added, forcing a smile to his lips.

He waited for her response, but it was David who spoke next. "Sounds great, Peter, but I'm booked on a flight that leaves in a couple of hours." He glanced at his watch. "I've just got enough time to get to the airport and go through security."

"Take a later flight," Peter urged.

He knew that David could well afford to pay the difference for changing his plans. The younger man was, after all, a highly sought after plastic surgeon. *People* magazine had referred to David as the surgeon to the stars in a recent article. He was certainly the family's success story—at least, financially. In contrast, Ella had just recently completed her residency. And God knew that he wasn't making a pile of money, Peter thought. About forty percent of his patients had no health insurance and could barely make token payments for their treatment, not that that would stop him from being available to them if the need arose.

However, Anna probably did quite well for herself in the business world. Her clothes certainly looked expensive, as did the car she drove. She never elaborated about her job, though, so it was left to Peter's imagination to fill in the blanks.

David shook his head. "You know I would, but I've got a surgery scheduled first thing in the morning. It was a last-minute booking," he explained. "Flying always tires me out and I need a good eight hours to be at my best." He paused for a moment, looking at his older brother. It was obvious that he did feel somewhat guilty about grieving and running. "Are you okay with that?"

No, Peter thought, he wasn't okay with that. But that was life. There was no point in creating a fuss, so he nodded and said, "I understand. Duty calls."

Squeezing through the opening that David had inadvertently left for her, Anna was quick to say, "I have to be going, too."

She deliberately avoided Peter's eyes, knowing that they would bore right through her, not that it really mattered. She'd come here for her father, not for any of them. She knew what they thought of her. She'd hoped that their father's passing might finally bring them together, but that obviously wasn't happening. In their eyes, she knew she would always be an outsider. There was no getting away from it.

"There's a meeting I need to prepare for," she told him.

She was lying, Peter thought. Anna always looked extremely uncomfortable when she lied.

But he wasn't about to press. "You'll be missed," he told her.

Now who was lying? he asked himself.

She debated leaving the comment alone and retreating while the going was good.

But she couldn't resist saying, "I sincerely doubt that." She saw both her brothers and Ella look at her in surprise. Was the truth that surprising? Or was it because she'd said something? "No one will even miss me."

"I will," Ella told her.

It was Anna's turn to be surprised. She looked at her sister. Only a year separated them and if she was close to anyone within the family, with the exception of her father, it was Ella. So much so that she'd taken time off from her impossibly hectic schedule to attend Ella's graduation. Aside from that, she'd only been home for the holidays and her father's birthday.

Now that he was gone, she doubted she'd be back at all. What was the point? There was no reason to return to this den of strangers. She had a feeling they would be relieved as well not to have to pretend that they cared whether or not she visited.

But for now, she smiled at Ella, grateful for the sentiment the youngest Wilder had expressed. Anna squeezed her sister's hand. "Thanks, El. But I still have to go."

"An hour?" Peter was surprised to hear himself say. Maybe it was the look on Ella's face that had prompted him to try to get Anna to remain. "Just stay an hour." He saw her reluctance to even entertain the suggestion. "For Dad, not for me."

"You can stay for both of us," David told her flippantly. Embracing Ella, he kissed his younger sister on the cheek affectionately, then gripped Peter's hand. "I'll be in touch," he promised his brother. And then he nodded at Anna, his demeanor polite but definitely cooler. "Anna, it was good to see you again."

Peter saw Anna's shoulders stiffen.

So much for a truce. Maybe some other time, he told himself.

He began to guide Ella to the parking lot and the limousine that had brought them here.

He didn't see Bethany Holloway approaching until she was almost at his elbow. Beautiful women occasionally captured his attention, and this woman was a classic beauty, with porcelain skin, luminous blue eyes and breathtaking red hair.

Wanting to get Peter's attention, Bethany lightly placed a gloved hand on his arm. Surprised, he turned to look in her direction.

"Oh Peter, I just wanted to say again how sorry I am about your father. Everyone loved him."

That much he knew was true. To know James Wilder was to admire him. His father had had a way of making people feel that they mattered, that he was actively interested in their welfare. In exchange for that, people would regard him with affection. It was a gift.

"Thank you."

He was trying to be gracious, but his words rang a little hollow. Maybe it was selfish, but for a moment, he wanted to be alone with his grief. And yet, he knew he couldn't. He didn't have that luxury afforded to him. No matter his emotions, he needed to hold it together so that everyone else could mourn as they needed to.

It certainly wouldn't help Ella cope with her grief if she saw him break down, he thought.

"But maybe," Bethany went on, falling into step beside him, "in a way this might have been easier for your father."

"'This'?" Peter echoed.

Bethany nodded. "His passing."

Peter stopped walking and looked at her sharply. He wasn't following her logic. "What?"

Bethany looked as if his reaction wasn't what she'd expected. "Think how Dr. Wilder would have felt, having Northeastern Healthcare take over."

Peter felt as if his brain had just been submerged in a tank of water. None of this was making any sense to him. "Take over what?"

Bethany looked at Peter in surprise. "Why, Walnut River General, of course."

Chapter Two

For a moment, it was so quiet Peter could hear the snow falling, the snowflakes touching down. He was only slightly aware that both Anna and David were still standing nearby.

"What are you saying?" Before Bethany could answer, he looked at Ella. His sister looked completely encased in her grief. He didn't want her subjected to anything more right now. "You look cold, Ella. Why don't you go on to the limousine and wait for us inside?" he suggested.

In a haze, Ella nodded and left the group.

Wilder hadn't heard, Bethany realized. What's more, he looked obviously upset by the news. She hadn't thought he would be. As far as she saw it, the proposed takeover was good news. Only people who resisted progress would view it as anything else.

Still, a qualm of guilt slid over her.

"I'm saying that it's official," Bethany explained. "NHC came out and announced that they were interested in acquiring Walnut River General." Her smile widened. "They're saying that it would be an excellent addition to its family of hospitals. Your father helped turn the hospital into a highly regarded institution, and he did a wonderful job," she added.

Maybe too wonderful, Peter thought. Otherwise, they would have continued operating under the radar.

"He didn't do it to have the hospital

pillaged by an impersonal corporation," Peter declared, feeling his temper suddenly rise. If he needed proof of the organization's insensitivity to the human condition, he had it now. The conglomerate was putting in a bid before his father's body was barely cold. "Those sharks wouldn't know what a family was if they were hit over the head with one."

"Don't hold back, Peter," David urged wryly. "Tell us what you really think."

Bethany glanced at the younger Dr. Wilder. She knew he wasn't part of the hospital staff, but she'd expected to hear something more in favor of what seemed inevitable than a joke. After all, a plastic surgeon, especially one of David Wilder's caliber, could appreciate a highly efficient organization.

Feeling slightly uncomfortable, like the bearer of bad news instead of good, Bethany cleared her throat. "Well, anyway, the board is going to be meeting tomorrow morning about this," she told Peter. "I thought I'd give you a heads-up, seeing as how this will be your first time and all."

She was referring to the position on the board he'd assumed. Not his father's position—that had gone to Wallace Ford. With Wallace assuming the chairmanship, that had left a seat open and, out of respect for James Wilder, the board had offered it to Peter. He'd accepted it out of a sense of responsibility and not without more than a little dread. He simply wanted to be a doctor. The seat on the board would get in the way, but for now he had no choice.

Peter nodded in response to her words, trying not to look as disturbed by the news as he felt. Right now, he was here for his father and that was all that mattered. There was time enough to worry about this newest development later.

"Thank you." Realizing how stiff he sounded, Peter made an effort to be more congenial. "Will I see you at the reception?"

A trace of Bethany's smile entered her eyes as she answered, "Of course.

Again—" she took hold of Peter's hand and looked up into his eyes "—I am very sorry for your loss." She glanced over toward the limousine where Ella sat waiting. "And your sister's," she added.

At least it was death that had taken the man from Peter and his siblings, she couldn't help thinking. Her parents had simply left her years ago—if they had ever been there to begin with.

A quick smile flashed across her generous mouth. "I'll see you later," she promised, and then she slipped back into the dispersing crowd as they all made their way to their separate vehicles.

David stood beside Peter for a moment, watching Bethany's back as she walked away. His thoughtful expression hinted that he was envisioning what she might look like beneath the white winter coat she had on.

"Well, that's a new face." He turned back to his brother, for the moment ignoring Anna's presence. "Nice structure. Good cheekbones."

Anna made a small, annoyed noise. "Do you have to look at everyone like a work in progress?" Her disapproval was evident despite the fact that she kept her voice low.

David's shoulders moved in a half shrug beneath his camel hair overcoat. "Sorry, occupational hazard. It's the artist in me. Although—" he addressed the rest of his remark to Peter "—there doesn't seem to be anything to improve on with that one. Who *is* she?"

"Bethany Holloway," Peter answered. His and Bethany's paths had crossed perhaps half-a-dozen times, perhaps less, since she had come to Walnut River. "She's on the board."

Mild interest traced itself over David's handsome features. "New member, I imagine. As I remember it, the board was a collection of old fossils."

Peter laughed shortly. "Not anymore. Things have changed since you left for the West coast. Dad's been the oldest one on the board for a while now. Or he was," he corrected himself. God, but it was hard thinking of his father in the past tense. "Some of the others retired.

"Bethany's an efficiency expert. She's been on the board for as long as she's been in town. About six months or so, I think." Peter thought of what he was going to be facing tomorrow. "I guess I'd better start becoming more involved with the business end of things now that I'm part of it."

David looked impressed. "You're taking over Dad's old seat?"

Peter shook his head. "No, not exactly. Dad was the chairman. I've got a long way to go before I'm experienced enough for that position—not that I want it," he added quickly. As far as he was concerned, being on the board was a necessary evil. "Dad always regretted how much time being chairman took away from doing what he really loved."

A comfortable silence hung between the two brothers for a moment. "They don't make 'em like Dad anymore, do they?"

And then David looked apologetically at his older brother. "No disrespect intended."

"None taken," Peter replied easily. "James Wellington Wilder was one of a kind. We shall not see his like again."

David rolled his eyes, his natural humor returning. "You're starting to quote Shakespeare, time for me to leave."

Peter hated to see his brother go. David was around so infrequently and there never seemed to be enough time to catch up. "Can I give you a ride to the airport at least?"

David shook his head. "I've got a taxi waiting." As if to prove it, he nodded toward the lot. Peter made out the yellow body and black lettering of a local cab service. "You know I hate long goodbyes."

Peter nodded. "I know it. Ella knows it."

"Don't worry about NHC," David advised.

Peter laughed shortly. "Hard not to," he said honestly. "What is their motto again? Whatever NHC wants, NHC gets?"

David grinned. His money was on

Peter. His brother might be a man of few
words, but in Peter's case, still waters ran
deep. Very deep.

"No, I think it's: 'We've never met a
dollar bill we didn't like'." He felt com-
pelled to give his older brother a few
words of encouragement. "Which is
exactly why Walnut River General won't
be joining their so-called family. People
feel cared for when they come to Dad's
hospital—excuse me, your hospital—"

"It's not mine," Peter corrected. "You
were right the first time. Dad's hospital."

David ignored him because they both
knew that wasn't true. Walnut River
General was the mistress in Peter's life, the
lover he lavished his attention on and from
whom he'd never strayed. Peter's life was
filled with relationships, but they were all
with his patients and friends. Not a single
one of them was a romantic entanglement.

From the moment he first took his Hip-
pocratic oath, Peter had been devoid of
any sort of relationship that might eventu-
ally become permanent. There'd been one

in college, but that was all behind him. Beyond caring about his own family, Peter had told David more than once that there wasn't time for anything else.

"You can't put a price on that," David concluded, as if Peter hadn't interjected anything. He paused to embrace his older brother before taking his leave. "It'll be all right." he promised. "Call me if you need me. I'm only a five-hour flight away—if you don't factor in inclement weather and mile-long security lines," David added with a grin.

Crouching for a moment, he peered into the limousine. Ella rolled down the rear window and leaned forward. "Make me proud, little sister."

Peter smiled, shaking his head. "Just what she needs, pressure."

David raised his shoulders and then lowered them in another careless half shrug. "We all need a little pressure." He glanced toward Anna as he made his pronouncement. "Keeps us on our toes and keeps life interesting."

Anna shifted uncomfortably as David told her goodbye again and then hurried off to the cab.

"I'd better be leaving, too." She looked at Peter, loathing to ask for a favor but she'd been so overwhelmed with grief, she hadn't been thinking straight when they set off to the church. "If you could drop me off at my hotel on the way back to your place, I would greatly appreciate it."

She sounded as if she was talking to a stranger, Peter thought. "No problem," he told her.

The limousine driver had popped to attention the moment they'd approached the vehicle, and he was now holding the rear passenger door open for them. Peter waited until Anna climbed in beside Ella, then got in himself.

"Are you sure you won't come to the reception?" Peter prodded. "Just for a few minutes."

But Anna remained firm. "I'm sorry, I really do have to leave. I have a flight to catch, too. I realize that I won't be reconstructing some Hollywood wannabe starlet's breasts in the morning, but what I do is important, too."

"No one said it wasn't, Anna," Peter pointed out.

Why did everything always devolve into an argument between them? Right now, he really wasn't in the mood to walk on eggshells.

Unable to take any more, Ella spoke up. "Please, we just buried Dad. Do you two have to do this now?"

Their father's death had brought everything too close to the surface. Like nerves and hurt feelings.

It was Peter who retreated first.

"Ella's right." It was on the tip of his tongue to say *We shouldn't be acting this way,* but he knew Anna would take the statement as accusatory and it would only add kindling to the fire. So instead, he changed the subject, hitting on what continued, thanks to Bethany's announcement, to be foremost in his mind. "Anna, I'm going to need your help."

It was obviously the last thing she had ever expected to hear from him. Anna looked at Peter, utterly surprised. "You need *my* help?"

He could feel Ella looking at him, mystified. But it was true. He did need Anna's help. "Yes."

This was definitely a first, Anna thought. An uneasiness immediately slipped over her. An uneasiness because she had a feeling she knew what her older brother was going to say. And if she was right, she was going to have to turn him down. Because she was facing a huge conflict of interest. So, she made a preemptive strike, nipping a potential problem in the bud before she was faced with it. "I'm sorry, Peter, but all my time is already accounted for over the next few months," she said firmly.

"I see." He let the matter drop, silently upbraiding himself. Given their distance recently, he should have known better than to ask.

Peter's small, two-story house was stuffed with people. Nearly everyone who'd attended the service and gone to the cemetery had followed the stretch limousine back to the reception.

Peter mentally tipped his hat to Ella. He had no knowledge of these kind of situations, no idea what was expected beyond the necessary funeral arrangements. Ella had handled all the subsequent preparations, securing a caterer and telling the man what to bring, where to set up and when.

Initially, when he'd seen how much food was going to be on hand, Peter had envisioned himself having to live on leftovers for the next six months. Watching his various guests help themselves, he smiled now, thinking that if there was enough left over for a sandwich for lunch tomorrow, he'd be doing well.

He supposed that sorrow brought out the hunger in some people. As for him, the exact opposite was true. He wasn't sure if he'd had more than a single meal since his father had suffered the fatal heart attack that had taken the man away from them.

Damn, but I am going to miss you, Dad.

You left too soon, he thought not for the first time.

"You're not eating."

The words took him by surprise. Or rather, the voice did. Bethany Holloway, the Jill-come-lately to the hospital's board of directors.

As he turned to look at her, he caught himself, thinking that David was dead-on in his evaluation of her appearance. But he had a sneaking suspicion that they might find themselves on the opposite sides of an opinion.

Pity, he thought.

"That's because I'm not hungry," he said, punctuating his statement with a half-hearted smile.

"You really should have something," Bethany advised. The next moment, she was putting into his hands a plate containing several slices of roast beef and ham that she had obviously taken for herself. "You're looking a little pale."

Trying to return the plate to her proved

futile. "You have a degree?" he asked amiably.

Bethany knew he meant in medicine, but she deadpanned her answer.

"In observation." She quickly followed up with, "And it doesn't take much to see that you haven't been visiting your refrigerator with any amount of regularity." That actually stirred a few distant memories within her. She really had so few when it came to her own home life. "My father used to get too caught up in his work to remember to eat," she added, hoping that might persuade him to take a few bites. She could well imagine how he had to feel. It wasn't easy losing family, and from what she'd observed of father and son, they had been close.

"Used to?" Peter echoed. "Is he—" He couldn't bring himself to finish the question. The word *dead* stuck in his throat like an open wound, the kind sustained by swallowing something that was too hot.

"Gone?" she supplied. It was a nice,

safe word for what he was implying, she thought. "No, actually, I'm the one who's gone. From the state," she added quickly when she saw his eyebrows draw together in minor confusion. "As far as I know, both of my parents are still working like crazy." Bethany lifted one shoulder in a quick, careless shrug and then took a sip from the glass of diet soda she was holding in her other hand. "It makes them happy so I suppose it's all right."

From her tone, Peter inferred that it was *not* all right with her. Questions about her began to form in his mind.

Bethany looked around the tightly packed family room and beyond. There was barely enough space for people to mill around without rubbing elbows and other body parts against one another.

"This a very large turnout." She smiled at him. "Your father had a lot of friends."

To know his father was to like him, Peter thought. "That he did."

"I didn't know him very well," Bethany began, picking her words carefully, "but

the little I did know, I liked a great deal."
Her smile widened and Peter caught
himself thinking that she had an extremely
infectious smile. "He reminded me a little
of Jimmy Stewart in *It's A Wonderful Life*,
always thinking about other people and
what they needed." She raised her eyes to
his and, just for an inkling, Peter thought
he felt something inside himself stirring,
reacting to the soft blue gaze. "You kind
of look like him." He perceived a hint of
pink along her cheeks. "I mean, like the
portrait of him that's hanging in the
hospital corridor outside the administra-
tion office. Same strong chin, same kind
eyes."

And then she laughed. "I'm sorry," she
apologized. "I always speak my mind. My
mother told me it would get me in trouble
someday." Lectured her, actually, but Peter
didn't need to know that.

"And has it?" he asked. "Gotten you in
trouble I mean."

She shook her head. "Not yet, but
there's still time." Bethany looked past his

shoulder. A curious expression slipped over her flawless features. "I think that man is trying to get your attention."

Peter turned to look over his shoulder and saw Fred Trinity, his father's lawyer. The latter looked relieved to make eye contact and waved him over.

What's this all about? Peter wondered. The formal reading of the will, not that it was really necessary, was set for tomorrow.

Well, he might as well find out, he thought. "If you'll excuse me," Peter murmured, handing her back the plate she'd given him.

"Of course." Bethany frowned at the untouched fare on the plate. "Don't forget to eat something," she called after him. And then, with a resigned sigh, she turned back to the crowd.

It took him a minute before he realized that he was just standing there, watching her walk away, thinking that the woman looked good going as well as coming.

Chapter Three

With his shaggy mustache and gleaming bald head, Fred Trinity looked like a walrus in an outdated suit that might have fit him well some twenty-five, thirty pounds ago. His carelessness, however, only extended to his appearance. His mind was as sharp as the point of a sword.

Placing a solicitous hand on Peter's arm, the lawyer lowered his voice, as if the weight of his words wouldn't allow him to speak any louder.

"Could I see you alone for a minute, Peter?"

The grave expression on the man's round, ordinarily amiable face was not reassuring. A chill passed over Peter's shoulder blades and he couldn't help wondering if this had anything to do with the threat he'd so recently been made aware of, the one posed by NHC. Fred had been his father's lawyer for as long as he could remember, but he wasn't the legal counsel that the hospital board turned to. Still, Fred might have been privy to some sort of inside information. Lawyers talked among themselves like everyone else, didn't they?

Bracing himself, Peter nodded. "Sure." He indicated the doorway leading to other parts of the house. "We can go to my study. It's just down the hall."

Crossing the living-room threshold, Peter led the way out.

"I've never been to your house before," Fred commented, looking around.

"It's not much of a treat," Peter confessed. "I'm afraid I've let things get away from me. You know how it is."

"Actually, no," Fred replied. "Selma handles all that. You need a wife, Peter."

"I'll put it on my list of things to do," Peter promised.

The house was older than Peter and in need of attention and a fair amount of updating. Other than hiring an occasional cleaning crew to do battle with the cobwebs and the dust, nothing had been changed since he'd moved in shortly after graduating from medical school. He honestly couldn't remember the last time he'd had the house painted, but then, he rarely spent much time here.

He was always at the hospital, either in the O.R., the emergency room or in his fourth-floor office. His house was just the place where he received his mail, did his laundry and slept. Beyond that, it really didn't serve much of a function.

Like the rest of the doors in the house, the door to his study was wide-open. He didn't like closed doors. Closed doors meant secrets. It was a holdover from his childhood. On the rare occasions when his parents would have words, the doors were always closed. When they were opened again, his parents would emerge, each with sadness in their eyes.

As he walked in, Peter flipped a switch on his desk lamp, which cast a dim light.

He switched the three-way bulb on high, then turned around to face the man he had ushered in.

"What's wrong, Fred?"

Fred looked somewhat uneasy. Peter couldn't remember ever seeing the lawyer look anything but comfortably confident. Fred reached inside the breast pocket of his jacket and took out a bulky-looking white envelope. Watching Peter's face, Fred held it out to him.

Across the front of the envelope, in his father's very distinct handwriting, was his name.

"Your father wanted me to give this to you. It was only to be opened in the event of his death," Fred explained and then sighed with genuine sorrow. It was no secret that he'd known James Wilder for over sixty years. They'd gone to school together. "Which is now. I am going to really miss that man. Did I ever tell you that he saved my life?"

Peter stared at the envelope before taking it. What could his father have written that he couldn't have said to him in person?

"Twice." A heaviness hovered over Peter as he took the envelope Fred was holding out. He had an uneasy feeling he didn't want to know what was inside. "When did he give this to you?"

"Five years ago. Shortly after your mother died." The man's small mouth curved beneath the shaggy mustache. "I think her death brought mortality into his life in big, bright letters. It hit him then that no one was going to go on forever, not even him, and he had some things he wanted to get off his chest, I suppose." Fred pressed his lips together. "Damn, I thought if anyone would have been able to cheat death, it would have been him."

"Yeah, me, too." His father was the most decent, honorable man he had ever known, as well as the most dedicated. There were no skeletons in his closet, no real deep, dark secrets. His father's life had been an open book. "What makes you think my father had something he wanted to get off his chest?"

"Because, for one thing, there are no letters for David or Ella or Anna. I guess as the family's new patriarch, he was turning to you." Fred's bushy eyebrows rose in surprise as he watched Peter tuck the letter into his own breast pocket without opening it. "Aren't you going to read it?"

Peter shook his head. "Not right now. I need to get through this ordeal first before I'm up to tackling another problem."

Fred nodded, but it was obvious he was curious about the envelope's contents. However, it wasn't his place to prod.

"Makes sense," Fred allowed. His mission accomplished, he took a step toward the doorway, then stopped. "By the way, is tomorrow evening still convenient for the reading of the will?"

Convenient. What a strange word to use under the circumstances. Peter took a breath, doing his best to block the barrage of sadness that threatened to overwhelm him again.

"Tomorrow evening will be fine, Fred," he replied quietly.

Fred continued to pause as another thought occurred to him. "What about Anna and David? I don't see either one of them at the reception."

"That's because they're not here," Peter replied simply. He could see the answer didn't please the man. Crossing back to the doorway, he turned off the light. "If there's anything out of the ordinary in the will—" which he was confident there wouldn't be "—I can always call and tell them."

Fred nodded as they walked out of the room together. "Rumor has it that NHC is about to come knocking on the hospital's door." He stopped short of the living room. "What are you planning to do about it?"

"Not answer," Peter replied with a finality that left no room for argument.

Fred grinned broadly and clapped him on the shoulder. He had to reach a little in order to do it. "Good man. You'd make your father proud." He lowered his voice again, assuming a conspiratorial tone. "He's watching over you now, you know that, don't you?"

Peter merely offered a perfunctory smile. He wasn't exactly sure how he stood on things like that. What he did know was he would have preferred to have his father at his side. Or better yet, leading this charge against the anticipated assault. James Wilder was far better suited to staving off the barbarians at the gate than he was.

But he was going to have to learn. And fast.

The first person Peter noticed when he walked into the boardroom the next morning was Bethany Holloway. Out of respect for the late chief of staff, she was wearing a black sheath. It made her hair seem more vividly red, her complexion ever more porcelainlike.

Black became her, Peter thought absently. On her, the color didn't look quite as somber.

The eight other board members in the room were also wearing black or navy, undoubtedly prompted by the same desire to show respect, Peter mused. His father would have been surprised at how many people mourned his passing. But then, the man had always been so unassuming, never thinking of himself, only others.

His thoughts momentarily brought him back to the envelope Fred had given him last night. He'd left it, unopened, on the mantel in the living room, unable to deal with its contents. He knew that was making assumptions, giving it an importance it might not actually have, but he couldn't shake the uneasy feeling that whatever was inside the envelope was going to change life for him as he knew it.

So for the time being, it was going to remain unopened. At the moment, he had enough windmills to tilt at. Especially if this threat posed by NHC actually was genuine.

The January sun had decided to make an appearance, pushing its way into the rectangular room via the large bay window that looked down onto the hospital's emergency room entrance.

Despite the brightness, Peter felt a chill zip down along his spine as he walked into the room. Everyone was already there. He was on time; they were early. Was there some sort of a significance to that?

Wallace Ford, the newly appointed chairman of the board, walked up to him and shook his hand as if he hadn't been at the service and subsequent reception just yesterday.

"Good of you to attend, Peter," he said heartily. Dropping his hand, he sighed heavily. "Again, let me express my deepest sorrow regarding your father." He cast a glance about the room before looking at Peter again. "We all lost someone very special to us."

"Thank you, Wallace, I appreciate that." Peter looked around at the other board members, all sitting at the long rectangular table. It seated twelve. Only nine seats were filled. He'd never paid attention to the exact number of board members before. There'd been no need. Maybe he should have.

Hindsight wasn't helpful.

"Where do you want me?" he asked Wallace.

Wallace gestured toward the chair beside Bethany. "Why don't you take the empty seat next to Ms. Holloway?" And then the chairman smiled at Bethany as if they were both in on a secret joke. "I guess you're going to have to relinquish your title as the newest member of the board, Ms. Holloway."

"Gladly," Bethany replied.

Wallace waited until Peter took his seat and then, running his fingers along the gavel he refrained from striking, the newly appointed chairman called the meeting to order and addressed the group.

"Because this is an impromptu meeting and we all have other places we need to be, I'm going to dispense with the reading of the minutes today and get right down to the heart of the matter." His small, brown eyes rested on Peter for a long moment. "Or matters, as the case might be," he corrected himself.

"First of all, we, the board and I—" Wallace gestured grandly around the table before continuing, and it struck Peter that the man was a born showman who was given to dramatic pauses "—would like to offer the position of chief of staff to you, Dr. Wilder."

For a moment, Peter didn't know what to say. Chief of Staff had been his father's position. In his later years, James Wilder juggled that *and* being chairman of the board. Both were full-time jobs. It never ceased to amaze him how his father managed to do justice to both, but he had.

In the end, it had probably taken a toll on his health.

That notwithstanding, Peter was flattered by the offer, but he knew his limitations. With a self-deprecating smile, he shook his head. "Thank you, all of you, but I don't believe I'm experienced enough to take that on."

Wallace laughed at the refusal. "Modest. You're your father's son all right. Actually, we're asking you to take the position on temporarily, just until we find a suitable candidate. Your father left very big shoes to fill. It's going to take us a while before we find someone who comes close to his caliber. Until then, we would consider it an honor, as well as a huge favor, to have a Wilder in that position for a little while longer." Wallace paused just long enough to allow the words sink in. "You'd really be bailing us out."

Very adroitly, the new chairman of the board had maneuvered him until his back was against the wall. Peter knew he had no choice but to agree. It helped somewhat knowing that it was only for a little while.

"Well, put that way, I don't think I can turn it down."

"Wonderful. Then it's settled. Peter Wilder is the new temporary chief of staff." Wallace grew somber, as if the next topic could only be spoken about with the utmost respect and gravity. "As for the second reason for this meeting, I think we're all aware of what that is, but I'll be the one to say it out loud. Northeastern Healthcare has expressed a great interest in acquiring our little hospital and I believe that their offer is worth discussing at length."

Peter could feel his stomach tightening. "As long as our final answer is no," he commented.

Wallace shot him a look as if he'd just violated some sort of sacred procedure.

He probably had, Peter thought. He wasn't up on the intricacies of parliamentary procedure and the kind of pomp and ceremony that went with conducting meetings properly. It had never aroused the slightest bit of interest in him.

What did interest him were people— patients—who needed his care, his skills. He couldn't help wondering how his father, a very simple man at bottom, had been able to put up with all of this.

Wallace narrowed his eyes as he continued to look at him. "Excuse me?"

Now that he was in the potential fray, he might as well speak his mind, Peter thought. "Well, you can't seriously be thinking about accepting their offer, Wallace."

Wallace frowned. "You haven't even heard the amount yet."

Peter laughed shortly. "I don't need to hear the amount. You can't put a price on what we do here."

"I'm sure that would come as a surprise to the insurance companies, Dr. Wilder," Bethany said. She saw the incredulous look on the doctor's face and quickly continued. She needed to make this man understand why he was wrong. "Patients pay for their care, that's the whole point. And if that care can come about more efficiently, more quickly, it's a win-win situation for us and for them." Her voice grew more impassioned as she continued. "Besides, we're just a simple hospital. One huge lawsuit could ruin us and force us to close our doors."

"There's never been a lawsuit against the hospital," Peter said, in case she was ignorant of the fact.

"That doesn't mean that there couldn't be," Bethany pointed out. "People are a great deal more litigation-crazy than they were when your father joined the staff here. With a conglomerate like NHC taking Walnut River General under its protective wing, we're all but invulnerable."

The other board members in the room faded into the background. One attempted to say something, but Peter ignored him. Because Walnut River General meant so much to his father, to him, this had suddenly become personal.

"And where does the patient fit in with

all this?" Peter wanted to know. How could someone who looked like an angel be so cold?

"The patient is the one who benefits," Bethany insisted. She clearly thought he was oblivious to that. "NHC puts us on the map, makes us eligible to receive grants, updates our equipment, perhaps even gets us state-of-the-art equipment. You can't possibly ignore that."

"No," Peter agreed. "Updated equipment is extremely important, but that's what we have fund-raisers for. And so far, they've done pretty well by us."

The man just wasn't getting the big picture. He thought too small. "Personal donations," she said. "Think how much more we could do with allotments from a conglomerate with bottomless pockets."

He wondered if she was actually that naive, or if it was a matter of her being heartless. He preferred thinking it was the former, but he had a feeling he was wrong. "Isn't that a little like selling our souls for thirty pieces of silver?"

Wallace cleared his throat, getting them to both look in his direction for a moment and breaking the growing tension.

"Aren't you being a little dramatic, Peter?" Wallace asked.

"No, I'm being pragmatic," he responded. "I didn't go to medical school to practice assembly-line medicine." His main focus wasn't Wallace, it was Bethany. He wanted to make her understand, to see the flaw in the way she thought. "The doctors here treat the whole patient, they don't deal with him or her piecemeal. I don't want some accounting analyst holding a stopwatch and looking over my shoulder, telling me that I need to move faster or I'll wind up pulling the hospital's batting average down."

"There's nothing wrong with seeing more patients," Bethany insisted.

"There is if you wind up shortchanging them because you have a quota to meet or a schedule to live up to. Can't you see that?"

Bethany's eyes flashed angrily. Was he

accusing her of being obtuse? She'd never reacted well to criticism. She'd had to put up with a lot of it while she'd been growing up. She didn't have to anymore.

"You're ignoring all the benefits that being part of an organization like Northeastern Healthcare can provide for the hospital. They have access to far more facilities than we do."

"Looks like someone has done their homework," Wallace said. There was no missing the admiration in his voice or the approving look on the chairman's face as he looked at Bethany.

Was Wallace for the takeover, or was he just trying to score points with Bethany? Peter wondered in mounting frustration.

He didn't often lose his patience, but his father's death had changed the rules and shaken him down to his very foundation.

"Then give her a gold star, Wallace, but don't give NHC the hospital. Everyone will regret it if you do, most of all, the patients." Peter rose from his chair. The legs scraped along the floor as he pushed it back from the table. "Now, if you will all please excuse me, I have patients waiting to see me."

It was only by calling up the greatest restraint that he didn't slam the door behind him as he left.

Chapter Four

Bethany could feel the vibrations created by Peter's exit long after he'd left the room. Even after the meeting had abruptly broken up less than fifteen minutes later. Until she'd witnessed Wilder's reaction she'd figured the takeover to be a slam dunk.

So much for intuition.

She wouldn't have thought it to look at him, but Wilder was positively archaic. The man was standing in the way of progress, pure and simple. He was obviously so stuck in the past, he refused to open his eyes and see the future, or even acknowledge, much less read the handwriting on the wall.

Bethany's mouth curved as she walked down the fourth-floor corridor. It looked like it was up to her to make the temporary chief of staff see the error of his ways. She'd made up her mind about that the moment the meeting broke up. All the other board members already had some sort of relationship with Peter and seemed obviously wary of upsetting him, whether because they liked him, or were still treading on eggshells because of his father's recent death. Just as possibly, their hesitation arose out of respect for the late James Wilder.

Whatever the reason, she didn't know and she didn't care. No single person should be allowed to stand in the way of bettering a situation that ultimately affected so many just because clearly he viewed all change as bad and something to be avoided.

She knew people like Peter, had dealt with them before. People so set in their ways they felt there was no true path except the one they were standing on. They were stuck there, like the prehistoric creatures had been in the La Brea tar pits. The only difference was, the animals hadn't wanted to be stuck—they'd wandered in and had no choice. Wilder had a choice and he'd focused on the wrong one.

Knowing she couldn't confront the man while he was seeing patients, Bethany positioned herself outside his office a few minutes before noon. She assumed that, like every other physician she had ever known, he would break for lunch around that time. So she waited.

At one o'clock, she was still waiting.

Mystified, Bethany moved to the door and tried the knob, intending to check whether Wilder was still actually in his office or had somehow managed to leave by a back door without her knowing it. Her hand was on the knob when the door suddenly opened. Jerked forward, she stumbled and found herself bumping up against the doctor full force.

He was quick to grab her by the shoulders so the collision wouldn't send her falling backward. Caught off guard, she sucked in her breath, stifling a noise that sounded very much like a gasp.

She wasn't accustomed to being at an awkward, physical disadvantage. She liked being in control. Complete poise had been her credo since college. To her credit, she managed to collect herself almost immediately.

"Oh, Dr. Wilder—"

"That's what it says on the door," he acknowledged, unable to see why she should sound so surprised at seeing him walk out of his own office. Ever the doctor, his dark eyes swept over her, checking for any minor signs of damage or bruising. There were none visible. Still, he asked, "Are you all right?"

"Yes." Bethany brushed absently at her dress, smoothing it out. "I'm a lot more resilient than I look."

"Good." With a satisfied nod of his head, Peter began to walk toward the elevator.

Bethany had expected him to stand still so she could talk to him. Instead, she had to fall into step to gain his ear. Moreover, she found she had to fairly trot in order to keep up with the man. If she didn't know better, she'd speculate that he was trying to avoid her.

"I was hoping to run into you—"

He glanced at her with mild, amused interest. "And you decided to do that literally?"

She frowned. Was he teasing her, or did it go deeper than that? Her childhood was steeped in ridicule and the wounds from that had never quite healed. "That wasn't the plan."

Stopping by the elevator, Peter pressed the down button on the wall. A faint glimmer of a light went on, circling the button.

"What *was* the plan?" he asked, feeling that he was probably setting himself up. Braced, he sank his hands into the deep pockets of his lab coat and waited for her to answer.

Bethany psyched herself up for exactly

half a second before saying, "I wanted to talk to you about NHC's offer."

He looked at her for a long moment. The woman didn't appear to be someone who had adult attention deficit disorder. But then, you just never knew, did you? From what he'd gathered, she was an overachiever. That could be a sign.

"I believe you already did," he reminded her.

"But you walked out," she countered. Walked out before she could even get warmed up, she added silently.

"Not very polite," Peter granted amicably. "But in all honesty, there was no point in wasting your time or mine. I'd heard enough."

"You hardly heard anything at all."

There they had a difference of opinion. "I heard the words 'Northeastern Health-care' and 'takeover.' In my book, that's really enough."

The man really *was* closed-minded, Bethany thought, annoyed. Which meant that she had her job cut out for her. But she was up to it. She liked Walnut River, liked working at the hospital. And she wasn't going to allow this man to stand in the way of the takeover.

Bethany did her best not to let her emotions surface as she argued. "You could at least listen to what they have to offer, Dr. Wilder."

"I'm not some hermit living in a cave, Ms. Holloway. I know exactly what NHC has to offer." He enumerated. "A lot of gleaming, brandspanking new equipment they ultimately resist letting us use because of the prohibitive cost of operating the same gleaming, brandspanking new equipment." The look he gave her felt as if it was going right through her, straight to the bone. "I'm not some child who can be bribed by the promise of an expensive toy."

The elevator arrived, empty. Peter stepped in. Bethany was close behind him. As the steel doors closed, she suppressed a sigh. Losing her temper was not the way to go.

"I don't think of you as a child, Dr. Wilder."

His mouth curved and she felt something within her responding to the expression. The man did have charisma, she couldn't help thinking. "I'm sure the medical board will be happy to hear that."

This wasn't funny and she didn't like being the source of his amusement. "But I do think of you as a throwback."

The smile remained as he arched an eyebrow. "Speaking your mind again?"

Bethany squared her shoulders. Her chin went up. "Yes."

Peter faced forward and shook his head. "It's not charming."

"I'm not trying to be charming."

"Good." He continued looking at the steel door before him. "Because you're not succeeding."

Knowing the value of temporary retreat, Bethany backpedaled. A little. "Maybe *throwback* wasn't the right word."

He nodded, watching the floors go by. "Maybe."

She stopped backpedaling. "But you have to admit, you're stuck in the past."

That got to him. He turned his head to look at her. "No, I am in the present." He felt his temper flare, something that very rarely happened. What was it about this woman that got his jets flaming? "And I won't give up this hospital without a fight."

It was her turn to appear amused. "That's a little melodramatic, don't you think?"

"Whatever it takes, Ms. Holloway." Peter faced forward again, mentally counting to ten. "Whatever it takes."

The elevator arrived in the basement and he got off. All he wanted to do was to get a bite to eat before he went back to seeing his patients. Bethany was interfering with the smattering of peace and quiet he was hoping for. He *knew* he should have brought his lunch with him and remained in his office. But there hadn't been anything in his refrigerator to bring. He needed to get around to shopping, and soon.

He spared her a glance as he walked into the cafeteria. "Are you planning to follow me around all afternoon, Ms. Holloway?"

Bethany responded with a wide smile, paraphrasing his earlier words, "Whatever it takes, Dr. Wilder. Whatever it takes."

He inclined his head. "Touché."

She grabbed at what she felt was a temporary truce. "Won't you at least listen to me?" she pressed, following Peter into the main area where all the food was served. There were steam tables on two sides of the opposite wall and a bed of ice for cold beverages and desserts on the third. Just before the exit were the coffee dispensers.

Peter picked up a tray and handed it to her. She looked a little uncertain as she accepted it.

"I'm assuming you want to keep up the ruse that you actually want to be here," Peter said, moving to the left wall. "That means buying some food."

"Right," she murmured. Bethany looked around the cafeteria. This was actually her first time down here. She usually left the grounds at lunchtime, preferring to get her meals at one of several nearby restaurants. "*Then* will you listen to me?"

"I've been listening to you since you pounced on me outside my office," he told her innocently.

His comment earned him an interested look from the young nurse who walked by, her tray laden with what passed for a nutritious lunch. The woman's hazel eyes went from him to Bethany and then back again before a very wide smile sprouted on her lips.

Terrific. "I think you and I just became the latest rumor that's about to make the hospital's rounds," Bethany noted glibly.

He nodded his head, as if that was fine with him. "They have little else to talk about this week," he said drily. Nodding at the small row of dispensers, he asked, "Coffee?"

Her attention was already drawn to

another dispenser beyond the quaint coffeemaker that contained the simple fare. "I'll take a latte."

"Of course you will." He supposed he would have been disappointed if she hadn't. It would have meant that he was off target about her. And he knew in his gut that he wasn't. "I should have known that."

She proceeded to fill her cup. "Lattes are something else you don't approve of?" she asked.

He heard the high-handed note in her voice but went on as if he was talking to a friend. "What I don't approve of is pretentiousness, or change for the sake of change and not because it's a good thing."

Bethany grabbed her tray and quickly followed him. He stopped by a display of already wrapped sandwiches and grabbed one without even noting what it was.

"If you're talking about the takeover, it *would* be a good thing," she insisted emphatically.

Peter made a low, disparaging noise to

show his contempt for the thought, not the woman.

"I've been to other HMOs, Ms. Holloway. I know the kind of medicine that's practiced there. I categorically refuse to see that happen here. At Walnut River General, we treat the whole patient. Not his arm, not his leg, not his liver, but the *entire* patient, no matter what his or her complaint might be."

That sounded good in theory, but it was a completely other thing in practice. "Don't you think that's rather time-consuming?" *Not to mention costly*, she added silently.

He knew she'd see it that way. This would be exactly the same argument he would be having over and over again with the administrators if they joined NHC. "Perhaps, but if you don't treat the entire patient, you might miss something very relevant and specific to his or her case."

"And how many times does that actually happen? Finding something that doesn't apply to anyone else with the patient's condition?" she challenged.

That would be the efficiency expert in her coming out, Peter thought. "More times than you would think." He paused to look directly at her. "Once is enough if it's you," he told her, his voice low as he placed a very personal point on the matter.

Okay, he was right, Bethany allowed as she followed him to the checkout area, but she was still willing to bet those kind of patients only surfaced once in a blue moon. The rest of the time it was business as usual.

"But in the long run—" she persisted.

Nodding a silent greeting at the cashier, Peter took out his wallet and indicated to the man that he was paying for both his and her selections. He handed the man a twenty.

"In the long run, we will keep on doing as much good as we have been," Peter told her firmly.

She saw the exchange of nods and money. Bethany was quick to take out her wallet from her purse. "I can pay for my own food."

Peter picked up his tray and walked away. "Never doubted it for a moment, Ms. Holloway."

"Thank you," she replied primly, grabbing her own tray and quickly following him into the dining hall. "Do you realize that you just said my name as if it was some sort of evil incantation."

He didn't bother turning around to look at her. "Maybe that's your guilty conscience making you think that."

"I don't have a guilty conscience," she said with more than a note of indignation managing to break through.

"I would. If I voted for the takeover." Finding a small table in the back, he made his way toward it and then placed the tray in front of him on the table before sitting down. "Fortunately, that isn't going to happen."

She stood at his elbow for a moment, frustrated. "And your mind is made up?"

"Yes."

She shook her head, her voice fraught with disappointment. "You know, I never thought you would be the closed-minded type."

"Life is full of surprises." He watched her place her tray opposite his on the table and then slide in.

"Why have you singled me out?" he wanted to know. "I'm just the newest member of the board." And as such, he thought of himself as having the least amount of influence.

But that wasn't the way she saw it. "Because you do hold a lot of sway. You're Peter Wilder, resident saint. Moreover, you're James Wilder's son, an even bigger saint in his day. People look up to you, and they respect you. If you feel strongly about something, people think there has to be a reason." She tried not to notice that his smile made her stomach tighten again.

"There is."

"And," she continued, valiantly pretending that he hadn't spoken, "they'll vote the way you vote."

His smile was a thoughtful one. "But not you."

She slowly moved her head from side to side, her eyes never leaving his. "I don't vote with my heart, I vote with my head."

"Pity." He could see that she was about to take exception to his response so he elaborated. "You know, most of the time the heart is a far better judge than the head." He took a sip of his coffee, then set down the container and leaned forward. "I'm curious. Why are you so set on this takeover happening, Ms. Holloway? What do you get out of all this?"

She didn't even have to think, didn't hesitate with her answer. "Progress."

Peter shook his head. "I don't see it that way." He glanced at his watch. He could better spend what little time he had left before he opened his office again. Placing his sandwich in a napkin, he wrapped it up. He rose to his feet, sandwich in one hand, the remainder of his coffee in the other. "Now, if you'll excuse me, I have somewhere else to be."

Her eyes narrowed. He was lying, she was sure of it. Why come all the way here, then sit down just to leave? "Where?" she challenged.

"Appointments," he told her with a smile. And then, turning on his heel, he walked away.

Stunned, Bethany glanced around to see if anyone near her had overheard the exchange between them and, if they had, were they now looking at her with a measure of pity?

Even though she didn't see anyone looking in her direction, Bethany squared her shoulders and raised her chin defiantly.

She'd spent most of her life, both as an adult and as an adolescent, striving to be the highest achiever, the one who consistently was successful in grabbing the brass ring. Once acquired, she always went on to the next prize because, she had discovered, the getting was far more exhilarating than the having. Victory was exciting for only a few minutes—after that, it was hollow.

She felt that way about everything. It

didn't stop her from hoping to someday be proved wrong.

But it hadn't happened yet.

Lifting the latte to her lips, she took a small sip, still watching Peter's broad shoulders as he made his way toward the exit, and ignoring the odd little flutter in the pit of her stomach as she did so.

He didn't know it yet, she told herself, but she was going to wear him down and win him over. He was the ultimate challenge and she had no intention of it going unanswered. A takeover really was in the hospital's best interest. It would put the hospital in line for advancements and most definitely for several lucrative study grants.

Right now, Walnut River General was just a quaint hospital, the only one in Walnut River, and while it had been nurtured to its present state by James Wilder and now had Peter Wilder overseeing it, what happened when the day came that there were no Wilders to render their services, to be the kindly country doctors that the hospital's reputation thrived on? Then what?

It took very little imagination on her part to envision conditions degenerating within the hospital to the point where it wouldn't be able to attract any physicians of high standing to join their staff. In the blink of an eye, Walnut River General could easily turn into a mediocre hospital staffed with mediocre physicians.

If NHC oversaw its management, that sort of thing wouldn't happen.

Besides, Bethany thought as she finished the last of her latte, these days no one fought city hall and won. That kind of thing just didn't happen anymore. If, indeed, it ever had.

She placed the empty container on her tray and carried both to the nearest conveyor belt. Stepping away, she dusted off her hands. Ready for round two.

It was damn time for Dr. Peter Wilder to realize that he had to stop standing in the way of progress before he and his precious hospital were left behind in the dust. The sooner she got him to acknowledge that, the sooner they could all move on.

Chapter Five

The reading of the will that evening at his house held no surprises. Fred arrived at seven, with Ella there a few minutes earlier, and it went as Peter had expected. All of his father's worldly possessions, the house, the small bank account, were to be divided equally among the children. James Wilder had no living siblings, no distant people he felt honor-bound to reach out to beyond the grave. A few mementos went to friends, worth more in

sentimental value than they were mone-
tarily, but most items were part of the very
small estate that was to be divvied up
equally.

His father had left the execution of it
entirely in Peter's hands.

"Short and sweet," Fred declared.
Finished, he placed the will on the
mahogany desk and rose to his feet. He
snapped the locks back down on his black
leather briefcase. "Still, it's a shame that
David and Anna couldn't have stayed one
more day to hear the reading of the will
for themselves."

Peter knew that Ella felt the same way
the lawyer did: that David and Anna
should have remained out of respect for
their father. In her own way, Ella was very
protective of her father and his memory.
But he knew that no disrespect had been
intended by his siblings. Both excuses
they'd given were thin, veiling the different demons David and, to an extent, Anna,
had to wrestle with. Nothing anyone in the
room could say would change that.

So he played down their absence and responded to Fred's comment with a half shrug.

"They each thought that there wouldn't be anything unusual about it," he said. "And pressing circumstances called them away."

Fred's expression said he would have expected more from the children of his close friend. He nodded toward Ella as he circumvented Peter's desk. "Lovely seeing you again, Ella. I hope the next time we meet, it will be under happier circumstances."

"Yes," she murmured softly with feeling, "so do I."

Peter saw fresh tears glistening in her eyes. It was going to take her a while to get over this, he thought. In the meantime, he could give her her privacy.

Placing himself between Fred and his sister, he volunteered, "I'll walk you out."

"Speaking of unusual…" Fred picked up the thread of their earlier exchange as they left the room. "Have you, um, you know—"

Peter shook his head. "No, I haven't 'um, you know' yet."

Fred eyed him as they walked slowly to the front of the house. "Afraid it might be something bad?"

Afraid. Maybe that was the right word after all, he thought. Something about the presence of the envelope made him uneasy. He didn't want anything changing his image of his father and he was afraid that whatever was in the envelope might do just that.

"Well, it can't be something good, now, can it? If it was, there wouldn't be this aura of mystery surrounding it. My father wasn't the to-be-read-after-my-death kind of person. Or at least," he sighed, shoving his hands into his pockets as he walked, "I wouldn't have said he was." *Until now.*

Fred looked at him, a sympathetic expression on his round face. "Only one way to find out."

Peter glanced toward the living room as he passed it on his way to the front door. The thick envelope was still resting on the mantelpiece, where he'd placed it after the reception. And where it was going to stay until he was ready to deal with it.

"Yes, I know. I'll get to it," he promised. He stopped at the door. The overhead fixture hanging down from the vaulted ceiling was on high, casting more light through the area than it ordinarily did. The added brightness only marginally negated the somber atmosphere and mood.

Fred's eyes met his and the man said, "Be sure to let me know when you do."

Peter didn't feel comfortable with that. "Whatever it is, it's my father's secret."

Fred laughed softly to himself. "And I was your father's lawyer—and his friend. He had no secrets from me," Fred told him significantly.

Peter looked at him sharply. "Then you know what's in the envelope?"

It was obvious that Fred was not about to say yes—or no. "I have my suspicions," he admitted.

If that was true, what was all this cloak-and-dagger stuff about? And if Fred knew, what, exactly, did he want to be informed about after the envelope was finally opened and its contents read?

"Then why—"

"Lawyer-client confidentiality," Fred was quick to cite the standard, one-size-fits-all defense. Fred patted Peter's arm. "Keep an open mind," he advised. "Remember, you're the son James trusted."

Peter thought of the envelope that contained a secret his father had all but taken to his grave. The secret that James Wilder hadn't shared with him in life. "Apparently not."

The look in Fred's brown eyes told him that he could all but read his thoughts.

"Think of it as not burdening you until he absolutely had to." Fred glanced at his watch and looked surprised at the hour. "Well, I need to go. Selma is holding dinner for me." He laughed, patting his ample stomach. "Sometimes, I wish she was a worse cook than she is. Then I wouldn't have this—" he searched for a descriptive word that wasn't entirely unflattering

"—robust physique. 'Bye, Ella," he called out, raising his voice. "And let me know once you break the seal," Fred said again, lowering his voice so that it wouldn't carry.

Fred let himself out and closed the door behind him. The next moment, Ella was entering the foyer.

"What was all that about?" she asked.

Turning around, Peter saw that she had managed to pull herself together. Ella was good at rallying. He had to stop thinking of her as his baby sister. She was a grown woman and a doctor to boot. That meant she could handle her own battles.

Still, something had him saying evasively, "Just lawyer talk."

"I thought Fred was finished with all that in your study."

"You know lawyers, they never stop." He could see that Ella wanted details, so he embellished a little, elaborating on what had actually been on his mind earlier. "He wanted me to draw up a will, now that I'm head of the family."

Ella drew in a breath, as if that could protect her from what she was thinking. She shook her head vehemently. "You're not going anywhere for a very long time, big brother." Peter was eleven years older than she was, which made him half brother, half father as far as she was concerned. And she intended to hang on to both halves. "I absolutely forbid it."

Peter laughed, amused. "I'll let Fred know."

Ella tucked her arm through his. "You do that," she agreed. "Meanwhile, let's go out to dinner. My treat."

He glanced at his watch. It was getting late. "Aren't you on call?"

She'd drawn the graveyard shift. "Not for another few hours."

He smiled fondly at Ella. He'd decided to open the envelope after she went home. But there was no hurry. The envelope wasn't going anywhere. "Then you're on. And I warn you, I have expensive taste."

"Sky's the limit," she declared with a nonchalant wave of her hand. "As long as the sky's hovering somewhere in the ten dollar neighborhood," she added, her eyes twinkling.

He laughed. "I'll get the coats, Rocke-feller."

"NHC is sending a man to negotiate with us at the end of the month," Bethany announced without preamble as she walked into the small, cluttered office within an office where Peter retreated when he wasn't either making hospital rounds or seeing patients in either the exam room or the E.R.

It was barely eight o'clock in the morning. His patients didn't start coming in until nine-thirty and he had yet to make his rounds of the three that he currently had staying at the hospital.

Looking up from the medical journal he was reading, Peter frowned ever so slightly. He was going to have to remember to lock his doors until his hours began officially. Not even Eva, his nurse/receptionist was here yet.

He looked at the redhead for a long

moment. "Don't you have someplace else to be?"

Determined to break through his resistance, Bethany gave him a very complacent smile. "Not anyplace more important."

So much for catching up on his reading before making his rounds, Peter thought. Putting a bookmark into the medical magazine, he let the pages flip closed and rose to his feet. "Well, you might not have anywhere else you need to be, but I do."

She shifted to block his way. Other people at the hospital might think of Peter Wilder as a kind, gentle man, but at the moment, she thought of him as a stubborn jackass. A sexy jackass, but a jackass none the less. "That's what you said yesterday in the cafeteria."

He looked undaunted. "And it's still true. I'm not a hundred percent certain what it is that some of the other members of the board of directors do with their time, but mine is better spent doing what I was meant to do—doctoring."

It wasn't exactly true. He knew that four of the members were doctors, just like he was. Senior members of the staff, they had full agendas to follow even when they weren't seated around the table, reviewing tedious budgets and constricting overall policy. He knew she was an efficiency expert, whatever that actually meant.

"I have hospital rounds to make," he told her, heading for the same door that she had breached a minute ago. "So, unless you want to spend the greater part of the next hour standing in the hospital corridor, waiting for me to finish seeing my patients, I suggest you get back to whatever it is you're supposed to be doing."

And with that, Peter made his second escape from the woman in as many days.

"What do you know about Bethany Holloway?"

Finished with his rounds, his office hours still more than half an hour away, Peter decided to swing by the chief administrator's office to get a little information that might ultimately help him outsmart the attractive board member.

Henry Weisfield looked up from a travel brochure he'd been wistfully perusing and pushed his bifocals up his long, straight nose to look at the doctor he still thought of as "James Wilder's boy."

He smiled, letting his mind wander for a second. "That if I were thirty years younger, I'd be actively pursuing her. Why?" Henry slid his thin frame forward on his chair, his gray eyes momentarily bright with questions. "Are you interested?"

You would think that by the time a man hit forty, people would stop trying to pair him up with someone. Peter had been badly disappointed with that route once, and had more important things to do than spend time risking a part of his being that modern medicine had not come up with a way to heal.

"Only in so far as wanting to know where she comes from and why she's here," he answered after a beat.

Leaning back again, Henry told him what he knew. "The woman has not one but two business degrees. Graduated with top honors from Princeton and is a real go-getter. Wallace is very taken with her," he added.

Peter thought of the way the chairman had fawned over Bethany yesterday. "I'm sure that's a hit with Wallace's wife."

"Your father thought she had potential, too," Henry remembered.

Not if he'd known that the woman would back a takeover by one of the larger HMO companies, Peter thought. "If she's so brilliant, why isn't she sitting on the board of some big-name organization? Why has she graced us with her presence here?"

"Good question." Henry nodded more to himself than to him. "My best guess is that it has something to do with not wanting to be a little fish in a big pond."

That made sense, he supposed. Peter wandered over to the window and looked down the four stories to the back parking lot. It was beginning to fill up. Employees were reporting for the morning shift; visitors were beginning to make their pilgrimages to see friends and loved ones in hospital rooms and outpatients were coming in for tests they most likely didn't want to take.

They were doing fine just as they were, Peter thought. They didn't need some bloated conglomerate coming in, telling them what to do.

Fisting his hands, he leaned his knuckles against the windowsill. "So she's taken over our pond and is trying to make a name for herself here, is that it?"

Henry thought before answering. "Sounds about right." And then he chuckled to himself. "I hear that you walked out on her in mid-sentence at the board meeting yesterday."

Peter turned around to look at him. "I had patients waiting."

Henry's smile told him he knew better. "No, you didn't. I checked your schedule. You left a full half hour before your first appointment."

Peter thought that was rather an odd thing for Henry to do, but then Henry had always been one to move to the tune of a different drummer. Eccentric, he was still an excellent administrator, able to find ways to cover expenses at the last minute time and again. Henry was one of a kind and Peter was fond of him.

So he leveled with the man. "I didn't want to lose my temper."

"Lose your temper?" Henry echoed with a short laugh of disbelief. "I would have paid good money to see that. I didn't know you even had a temper. Most of the staff thinks of you as patience personified."

Peter felt himself chafing a little. Yesterday, Bethany had referred to him as a saint. Henry was telling him that the people at the hospital thought of him as the soul of patience. Deep down, he knew he was neither. He was just a man trying to do the best that he could at any given time.

Peter sighed. "I am what I need to be at the moment."

Henry leaned forward and peered at him

through the bottom of his glasses. "And right now, you seem a little—" Feigning surprise, he splayed his somewhat gnarled hand across his chest. "My God, you're a little annoyed." And then he smiled. "And this has to do with Ms. Holloway?"

Peter nodded. He had no idea why she rubbed him the wrong way so hard. Ordinarily, he took annoying people in stride. "The woman is a cheerleader for Northeastern Healthcare."

Henry sobered a little, but looked at Peter sternly. "Northeastern Healthcare is not the devil, you know."

Peter looked at him in surprise. He'd expected to find an ally in Henry of all people. "Henry, you don't mean that."

Rather than retract or retreat, Henry shook his head. His expression mirrored the confusion Peter felt inside. "Oh, I don't know," the older man said with a sigh. "Maybe I do. Maybe we're looking at the face of progress and by digging in against it, we might be turning our backs on something really worthwhile."

He had no idea what might have caused Henry to say that, but he knew in his soul that the man couldn't possibly mean it.

"What's worthwhile is good patient care. You know that, Henry. You don't have to be a doctor to know how going the extra mile can mean the difference between saving a patient and overlooking symptoms in the interest of the almighty profit margin."

Whether Henry was playing devil's advocate or had been brainwashed, Peter had no way of knowing when the administrator said, "The doctors at NHC aren't all soulless creatures."

Peter was willing to make a concession only up to a point. "Maybe not, but the organization that they work for won't allow them to access that part of themselves." He blew out a frustrated breath, feeling the base he was counting on eroding right beneath his feet. "Let them go take over some other hospital. We're small—barely a blip on their radar. Why the interest all of a sudden?"

Henry looked surprised by the question. "Don't underestimate what your father accomplished here. How hard he worked to make sure that Walnut River General was not just up to par, but above and beyond that in every possible way. Before James came on board, this was just 'a blip' as you called it. But not anymore. Definitely not anymore."

But Peter saw it another way. "If we were all that good, David would be here instead of practicing on the West coast."

"David's not here because he and your father came to loggerheads and they never patched up their differences," Henry reminded him. "And besides, maybe we're just less vain than the patients he finds in Los Angeles." Henry glanced at the latest quarterly bulletin that the hospital had released. On the front was a list of names of the physicians on staff. "We have excellent cardiologists, excellent orthopedic surgeons and even an oncologist who graduated from Yale."

Would those same doctors remain if the NHC took over? Peter had his doubts. "Then why would we need NHC?"

It was a tired voice that answered him. "Because we need new equipment." Henry sighed. "We need a lot of things."

Peter looked at him incredulously, still unable to believe what he was hearing. "So you're advocating the takeover?"

Henry shrugged. His head hurt. He'd been thinking of nothing else and waffling ever since the rumors had begun. "I'm advocating retirement. Mine," he clarified.

It was the last thing Peter had expected, or wanted, to hear. "Henry, no."

"Yes," Henry said gently. "I'm old, Peter. Older than your father was." A lot older, he thought. "And I'm tired. Tired of wrestling with hospital policies, tired of wondering how we're going to be able to fund this program or that—"

Peter cut in. "You've always done a fantastic job. We all thought you were part magician."

"It's time for someone else to pull a rabbit out of a hat," Henry said wearily. He loved the hospital, loved the people who were there, but his health wasn't what it used to be and it was suffering. He couldn't do as good a job as he had been doing and he refused to be in a position where the board voted to release him from his contract. "To struggle and lose sleep over ends that just refuse to meet."

Peter looked at the man closely. Henry did look tired. And there had been that late-onset diabetes that he knew Henry felt confident no one knew about. But he did. That was why he didn't press, even though he wanted to.

Still, he had to ask, "Your mind's made up?"

"About the retirement? Yes. About everything else? No." Henry shook his head again. "In theory, I agree that NHC should keep its sticky fingers off us. But we're not going to do anyone much good if we have to close our doors because the funding's not there to keep us going. Doesn't matter how good our reputation is if we can't get supplies because there's no money. Even when we don't charge some of the poorer patients who can't afford us, the services aren't really free, you know. Somebody has to pay for everything from a swab to a suture to everything else. Every department wants more and I just can't find a way to get it."

Peter squared his shoulders, as if ready to do battle with some invisible force. "I refuse to believe that HMOs are the only answer."

"Maybe they're not," Henry gladly conceded. "But I for one don't have any other answer." He rocked back in his chair. "Except to retire."

Resigned to the inevitable, Peter asked, "So, how soon?"

Henry glanced at the calendar on his desk and flipped a few pages. He was grateful that Peter wasn't calling him a coward and accusing him of running away from the battle. "April, maybe May. I've already half been scouting around for a replacement."

Whoever came wouldn't be nearly as good, Peter thought sadly. "Won't be the same without you."

Henry smiled, appreciating the kind words but knowing better. "You'll manage, Peter. You're a Wilder. The Wilders always manage."

The man's words echoed in Peter's head long after he'd left Henry's office. He knew his father had felt that way, as had his grandfather. He only wished he could feel half as confident about it as they had.

Chapter Six

It was hard not to fidget. Even harder not to let his eyes shut.

Peter couldn't help thinking he had more important things to do than sit here, trapped in this airless room, held prisoner by what felt like an endless board meeting.

For the better part of the week, his schedule had been entirely filled with patients. The rest of the time Peter found himself looking over his shoulder in an attempt—successful for the most part—to duck the very woman that fate now had him sitting next to in this so-called official meeting of the board of directors.

Larry Simpson, the current board secretary, had all but put him to sleep, reading the minutes in a voice that could, hands down, easily replace the leading medication for insomnia.

Part of the reason he was struggling to keep his eyes open was because he'd put in an extra long day yesterday. It had actually extended into the wee hours of the next morning—today. Too exhausted to drive home, he'd slept in his office. It had seemed like a good idea at the time, but the misshapen sofa was not the last word in comfort. He was now paying for his impulsive choice with a stiff neck, not to mention the various other parts of his body that felt less than flexible today.

After Larry had finished droning on, the first order of business had been the formal announcement of what he was already privy to: Henry Weisfield's pending retirement. That led to an impromptu testimonial by Wallace during which he listed Henry's skills and accomplishments.

"He's going to be a hard man to replace," Wallace predicted, using the exact words he had employed when he'd spoken about the passing of James Wilder. "But I charge each and every one of you to keep your eye out for a suitable candidate to at least partially fill Henry's position."

"We could try offering Henry more money," suggested Gladys Cooper, a fifteen-year veteran of the board.

"Not everything is solved with money." The words slipped out of Peter's mouth before he realized he was actually saying them aloud rather than just thinking them.

"No," the redhead at his elbow agreed. "But it certainly does help pave the road and make things a lot easier."

Not wanting to get caught up in another confrontation with Bethany, Peter replied, "Can't argue with that."

"Oh, I'm sure you can," she countered with a smile he couldn't begin to fathom.

Damn, but he wished she'd stop wearing that perfume. It wasn't overpowering. It was very light, actually, but it left behind just enough scent to stealthily slip into his senses, blurring things for him.

He had opened his mouth to respond when the sound of a cell phone playing a shrill samba reverberated through the room. The next second, Wallace's wide hand covered his jacket breast pocket.

"Sorry," he apologized with a sheepish expression. "Forgot to turn off my phone." But when he took it out to shut off, he looked at the number on the tiny screen. His expression turned to one of curiosity. He held up his hand as if to beg an indulgence. "I need to take this. Why don't we just take a break for a few minutes?" he suggested. Not waiting for the members to agree, he quickly left the room.

Everyone around them rose from their chairs, taking the opportunity to stretch their legs. Bethany watched the man at her left for a cue. Now that she had him in her sights, she intended to follow his lead in order to finally be able to say more than a handful of words to him regarding the takeover.

Peter remained seated. So did she.

"You didn't go home last night, did you?" Bethany asked quietly.

The question caught him off guard. But then, he thought, it really shouldn't have, given the fact that she had been popping up all over since Monday. "Are you stalking me, Ms. Holloway?"

She maintained a mild expression, as if tracking him down had never even crossed her mind. "No, I just noticed where you were parked when I left last night." She didn't add that she'd waited a quarter of an hour, hoping he would appear, since it was already after-hours. But sitting in her car on a cold January evening was her limit. "It snowed last night."

Where was she going with this, he wondered. And why did she have to look so damn attractive going there? "So I hear."

"You car had snow all around it this morning—as if it hadn't been moved," she said, explaining how she'd come to her conclusion.

"Very observant." Peter looked at her for a long moment, wondering whether to be amused or annoyed.

She smiled and something definitely responded within him. He vaguely recognized what was going on. This wasn't good, he thought.

"Look, Dr. Wilder, let's talk openly. What will it take to get you to listen to arguments for the other side?"

All around the table, people had begun to return to their seats, drawn in by the verbal duel.

He tried to make it as clear to her as he could. "You can't possibly tell me anything about NHC's motives that I don't already know."

Oh yes she could, Bethany thought. She had access to the latest studies, something she highly doubted this throwback bothered with. "There are statistics, Dr. Wilder."

He waved her words away with an impatient hand. "I deal in patients, Ms. Holloway, not statistics."

"Patients *make up* the statistics, Doctor," she insisted, and felt color rising in her cheeks. "Where do you think they come from?"

He banked down his impatience. The woman probably didn't know any better. Wiser people than she had been led astray by the hocus-pocus of numbers if they were juggled just right.

"Ms. Holloway," he began in a patient, quiet voice, "statistics are very flexible. In the hands of someone clever, they can be bent to support almost anything. The good done by a bloated, fat-cat conglomerate, for instance."

Her eyes blazed, reminding him, he suddenly realized, of Lisa. Of the woman he'd once thought—no, knew—he'd been in love with. The one he'd made plans to spend the rest of his life with. The one who'd left him in his senior year for a medical student who was "a better prospect" because once *Steven* graduated, he was slated to join his father's lucrative Manhattan practice.

A chill worked its way down his spine as the realization took root. Bethany Holloway had the same coloring, the same full lips, the same slender figure.

And the same take-no-prisoners ambition, he thought.

"Everyone I know at the hospital thinks that you're this kind, gentle, understanding man," she retorted. "So far, I'm not convinced they're right."

At that moment, the silence in the room was almost deafening.

And then Peter said quietly and with no emotion, "I have no desire to convince you about anything that has to do with me, Ms. Holloway."

But he knew it was a lie. What people thought of him did matter to him. He didn't like being thought of in a bad light. It bothered him.

Bothered him, too, that the sensual fragrance she always wore was really filling up his head, undermining his senses. It gave her an unfair advantage because it made him think of her during the course of the day when his mind was supposed to be on other things. And then his mind would wander. Wander in directions he was determined not to take. Not with her.

Where was all this coming from? Peter silently demanded. He was arguing to preserve the hospital, not fantasizing about his opponent. He wanted to save the place that had been a second home to James Wilder. Walnut River General was his father's legacy. And if NHC came into the picture, that legacy would be changed, if not eradicated entirely.

And Peter needed to do everything he could to keep that from happening.

"Sorry, sorry," Wallace announced, coming back into the room. He made a show of turning off his phone. "I hope you all got to stretch your legs for a moment, before we launch into part two of our agenda this morning." He chuckled at some joke he thought he'd made, then paused, waiting for the stragglers to be seated. Moments later, he began again. "First up, I'm told that the radiology department desperately needs a new MRI machine. The old one, according to Mrs. Fitzpatrick, the department's head technician, has been down more than it's been up in the last few months. Any ideas?" he asked, looking around the table as he threw open the matter for discussion.

He no sooner asked the question than Bethany's hand went up. The chairman nodded toward her. "Yes, Ms. Holloway?"

"If we take NHC up on their offer when they formally present it, we won't have to worry about how to pay for the new MRI machine. The money—" she slanted a look in Peter's direction "—would come from them."

"Yes, but at what price?" Peter countered, struggling to keep his temper in check. This should have been a no-brainer, if not for her, because of lack of experience, then for everyone else seated at this table. They all knew what HMOs, no matter what they called themselves, were like.

Obviously trying to keep the peace, Wallace asked him, "What do you mean?"

Was the man playing dumb for Bethany's sake? Heaven help him— maybe it was the lack of sleep talking— but he had no patience with that. "You know what I mean, Wallace. We've all heard horror stories about HMOs—"

"Yes, but those are all from the nineties and earlier," Bethany cut in. "Things have changed since then."

"Have they?" Peter challenged. "Instead of sitting around, waiting for NHC to come sniffing around, why don't we investigate some of the other hospitals that have become part of their conglomerate in, oh, say the last five years or so? See what they've become in comparison to the way they were."

Wallace cleared his throat uncomfortably. "Our resources are limited, Peter," he protested. "We can't afford to do that."

Didn't the man understand? If he was going to actually entertain this proposition, then he needed to know what might happen to Walnut River General.

"We can't afford not to," Peter insisted. "Now, as for the new MRI machine—" he knew how costly those could be "—why don't you have Henry Weisfield put together one of his fund-raisers? He's still not leaving for another three months or so. He could do it easily."

"That's your answer?" Bethany demanded, her voice rising. "A fund-raiser?"

The angrier she seemed to get, the calmer he became. "It's worked so far."

"And when we need to modernize the operating rooms?" she posed. "What then? *Another* fund-raiser? Just how many of these things do you think we can swing before we wind up losing donors altogether?" she asked.

"We'll tackle that when it comes," he said, smiling.

Was he laughing at her? "If NHC oversaw us, we wouldn't have to tackle anything. We would just make the request in writing."

He looked at her, stunned, not really sure she believed what she was saying. Was she just saying it to convince the others?

"Are you really that naive? Don't you realize that a company big enough to give you *everything*, is also big enough to take everything away if you don't dance to the tune they play?" He was tired of this. He was beginning to understand why Henry felt the way he did, why he wanted to retire. "If I'm going to have my strings pulled, I want to be able to see who's pulling them." He addressed his words to Wallace, not Bethany. With Wallace he had some hope of getting through. "Not having some conglomerate versed in buck-passing doing it."

Just then, his pager went off. Glancing down at the device clipped to his belt, Peter angled it so that he could read the message that had just come in. "Sorry, Wallace." He rose to his feet. "There's been a car accident. I'm wanted in the E.R."

Wallace nodded. "Of course."

As he left, Peter couldn't help thinking

that the chairman sounded rather relieved to see him go.

"Talk to me," Peter urged the E.R.'s head nurse, Simone Garner, a slender woman with brown hair and a ready smile, when he arrived in the emergency room several minutes later. As he questioned Simone, one of the other nurses helped him on with the disposable yellow paper gowns they all donned in an effort to minimize the risk of spreading infections amid the E.R. trauma patients.

The paramedics had left less than two minutes before, so Simone quickly recited the vital signs for the three patients, then added, "It was a two-car collision. The police said the brakes failed on the SUV and it plowed into the other car at an inter-section."

"Where did it happen?" he asked as he took out his stethoscope.

"Less than two miles away. The paramedics got them here quickly. Those two were the drivers." She indicated the first two gurneys. "The little boy was a passenger. Sitting in the front, I gather." The little boy was crying loudly. She pushed her hair out of her eyes with the back of her wrist and leaned in closer. "It's going to be all right, honey," she told him, then raised her eyes to Peter's face. "No child seat in the car," she said. It was obvious what she thought of the driver's negligence. "I think the little guy got the worst of it. He's pretty banged up. There might be internal bleeding."

"Get him to X-ray as fast as you can," Peter instructed. She motioned to an orderly and, between them, they took the gurney away.

Peter turned his attention to the other two victims. Before he could say anything, the man on the gurney closest to him grabbed his forearm.

"My little boy," the man implored hoarsely.

Peter looked down into a face that was badly cut up and bruised. One of the man's eyes was swollen shut and he looked as if he was barely able to see with his other one.

"Your son's going to be all right," he said with the conviction he knew the patient needed to hear. Long ago he'd been told not to make promises he might not be able to keep, but he knew the good a positive frame of mind could do. "Now let's make sure that you are." He pointed to the first empty bed he saw. "Put him in trauma room two."

He'd had to remove the boy's spleen. Then he'd gone back to the boy's father to explain at length everything that had been done. It had taken a lot to make the man believe his son was going to make a full recovery. Peter had never seen such concern, such guilt, displayed by anyone the way it was by Ned Farmer.

Farmer, a self-employed auto mechanic and former racer, berated himself over and over again for being so busy working on other people's cars that he'd neglected to check out his own.

"My fault, my fault, it's all my fault," Farmer kept saying over and over again, working himself up almost into a frenzy. It got to the point that Peter finally authorized an injection of diazepam be given in order to calm Farmer down.

The other driver, it turned out, had some traumatic bruising to his spine. So much so that the swelling was pinching his spinal cord, causing his lower extremities to become numb and unresponsive.

He called Ella and asked her to come down for a consultation. He thought his sister's soft voice and gentle manner might help quell the second driver's fears. She was there within the quarter hour.

The last he'd seen, Ella was at the man's bedside, calmly reassuring him. "In ninety-nine cases out of a hundred, the victim walks as soon as the swelling on his spine subsides. You just have to be patient."

The man looked anything but that. "But I'll walk again?"

"Most likely, as soon as the swelling there goes down," she repeated.

"But what if it doesn't?" he pressed nervously. "What if it doesn't go down?"

She took his hand in hers and said without wavering. "We'll do everything we can."

Peter smiled to himself and thought how proud his father would be if he could see her.

NHC, Peter was certain, would never approve of all this handholding on the part of their doctors. The patient would be swiftly examined, given his diagnosis and then sent home to recuperate. And to nurse fears of never being able to walk again. Who knew how much damage that would ultimately create?

It made him more determined than ever to block the takeover.

All in all, Peter thought as he changed back into his street clothes in his dimly lit office, this had been one of the worst Januarys he'd ever experienced.

He remembered Bethany saying it had snowed, and wondered if he was going to have to shovel his driveway when he got home that night. It wasn't a heartening thought. Despite having lived in Walnut River his whole life, Peter was definitely not a fan of the white stuff.

He paused just long enough to locate some lab and radiology reports and place them in his briefcase. When he stepped into the elevator car, it was empty. He continued to have it to himself all the way down. The doors opened again on the first floor and he walked out, then made his way down the corridor leading to the parking lot.

As he opened one of the double doors and emerged into the frigid night air, he was in time to hear a woman exclaim, "Oh damn," and then see Bethany Holloway suddenly disappear from view as she slid down the icy stairs.

Chapter Seven

Working triage in the E.R. had honed Peter's reflexes. Instinct just took over.

Holding on to the banister, he sailed down the steps and grabbed Bethany's arm just before her body came in ungraceful contact with the icy ground.

With her feet sliding in one direction and her body being jerked in another, Bethany overcompensated. In an effort to regain her balance, she threw her weight forward.

The next second, instead of keeping her steady, Peter found himself going down. He landed flat on his back. Since he was still holding on to her arm, he wound up pulling her down as well.

Right on top of him.

The air knocked out of her, she stared down at his face, stunned. He thought she'd indignantly scramble to her feet—or try to. Instead, she started to laugh. Her laugh, low, melodic and sensual, was highly infectious, not to mention that he could actually feel her laughing.

Picturing how absurd this had to look to anyone passing by—mercifully, there was no one—Peter started laughing, too. He laughed so hard, he became practically helpless and moisture began forming in the corners of his eyes.

Moving with the rhythm of laughter, their bodies rubbed lightly against each other.

Slowly, the laughter died away.

Caught between amusement and concern, Bethany struggled to regulate her breathing. "I don't think that this is what you had in mind."

Looking up at her, Peter found himself fighting an urge that hadn't come over him in a very long time. So long that he could barely remember the last time. The pace he'd kept up these past ten years had left very little time for him to even attempt to nurture a private life. Even if that was partly by choice.

Right at this moment, with her breath drifting down along his face and their bodies pressed together, he was acutely aware of what had been missing from his life. What *was* missing.

So aware that he wasn't conscious of anything but the tightening of his groin, the long, warm tongues of desire traveling through his body, heating it.

Making him yearn.

The look in her eyes told him he wasn't alone here. For whatever reasons, Bethany was experiencing the very same thing. The same attraction, the same electricity.

He wasn't a reckless man by nature.

Acting on impulse was something other men did, not him.

Until now.

In one unguarded moment, Peter reached up and framed her face with his gloved hands. He brought her face down to his.

If having her body on top of his had set off a series of sharp, demanding electric shocks, kissing Bethany multiplied the sensations tenfold. She tasted of fresh strawberries and spring, both equally far removed from the moment.

He lost himself in the sensation.

For one brief shining second, he wasn't Dr. Peter Wilder, highly respected internist, keeper of his father's flame. He was just Peter, a flesh-and-blood man who longed for companionship, for someone to be there for him at the end of the day, for someone with whom he could share his thoughts, his plans. His love.

He remembered other dreams he'd once had.

Her head was spinning so badly

Bethany thought maybe she'd hit it when Peter had accidentally pulled her down. But she'd landed on top of him and, though his body felt solid and hard, she knew for a fact that her head hadn't made contact with him.

Her pulse accelerating, she could almost feel her blood, exhilarated, surging through her veins.

Bethany deepened the kiss.

The second their bodies had come in contact, it'd felt as if something had just come undone within her.

But if she didn't draw back, if she let him continue even for another moment, Bethany was sincerely afraid of what that might do to her resolve, to the walls she'd been building up around herself for longer then she could remember. She only knew that they had been forged to keep the hurt back. If she let no one in, then she would never be hurt, it was as simple as that. She'd be invulnerable, the way she wanted to be.

She wasn't invulnerable now, she

realized. She was shaking. Inside *and* out. Any second now, it was going to occur to him that the cold weather had nothing to do with her reaction.

Her mind scattered in all directions, searching for something plausible to say in order to throw his attention off.

"So." The single word swooped out of her mouth on a breath that was all but spent the moment she drew her head back. And then she smiled down at him. "About that takeover."

She felt the laughter rumble in his chest before it burst from his lips. The up-and-down movement was soothing and erotic at the same time. So he did have a sense of humor, she thought, relieved. Thank God for small favors.

"One takeover is about all I can handle right now," he told her amicably. It was obvious that he wasn't talking about NHC—he was referring to what had just happened between them.

Confusion, enhanced by nerves, echoed in her head. The only thing she was certain of was that she wanted to kiss him again. She was even more certain that she shouldn't.

Placing his hands on her arms, Peter gently moved her back so he could sit up. When he did, he drew in a long, deep breath, then exhaled. Slanting a look at her, he apologized. It seemed like the thing to do.

"I'm sorry about that."

"Are you?" Was he sorry that he'd kissed her? The second she thought that, she felt this odd pinpricking sensation around her heart. What *was* that? Rather than deliberate over it, she struggled to block it.

Peter's eyes held hers. "The fall," he clarified.

Her breath had stopped in her throat and she had to force it back out again, had to consciously make herself breathe.

"And the kiss?" she asked softly.

Peter slowly moved his head from side to side. "I'm not sorry about that."

She looked at him for a long moment.

He wasn't lying, she realized. An unexpected wave of happiness suddenly drenched her.

"I'm not, either," she confided. And then she smiled at him, really smiled. "Finally, something we can agree on." Was it her imagination, or had his smile just deepened?

"I have something else we can agree on," Peter told her.

A leeriness slipped in again. She reminded herself that this was the man who opposed her ideas, whom she had to win over. She knew he was no pushover.

"Oh?"

He nodded. "That we should get up before someone comes by and sees us."

A wave of regret came and went. She couldn't begin to understand it. "Right."

Bethany was about to spring to her feet, but he was faster. Standing up, Peter extended his hand to her. She looked at it, then raised her eyes to his face.

"Isn't this what got us in trouble in the first place?" she reminded him.

He continued holding his hand out.

"Lightning rarely strikes in the same place twice."

She had a wealth of extraneous knowledge in her head, retaining everything she'd ever read, even in passing. "That's a fallacy, you know. Lightning's been known to strike twice in the same place. Sometimes even three times."

"I said 'rarely,'" Peter pointed out, trying to keep a straight face, "not 'never.'"

"Good enough." Wrapping her long, slender fingers around his hand, Bethany held on tightly as she rose unsteadily to her feet. Once up, she took a step and felt her feet begin to slide dangerously beneath her. Instantly her hand tightened on his. She wasn't pleased about coming off like some damsel in need of rescuing. "This is what I get for not wearing my boots," she murmured under her breath.

"I'll walk you to your car," he offered. "I'm not in any hurry." *For once*, he added silently.

She had an independent streak that was a mile wide and she considered it one of her chief sources of pride. It almost made her turn him down. But she also possessed more than her share of common sense and, in this case, common sense trumped independence.

So Bethany murmured, "Thank you," and then tried to make light of the situation by adding, "I've always depended on the kindness of strangers."

He looked at her and she could all but feel his eyes delving into her. He was probably wondering what she was talking about, she thought. And then he surprised her by commenting, "*Streetcar Named Desire.* You're a lot younger than Blanche DuBois."

She nodded, impressed. "You're familiar with the play?"

The corners of his mouth curved in amusement. "We're not entirely backward here. Town's got a library with books on the shelves and everything."

She hadn't meant to insult him, or be patronizing. It was just that she wasn't accustomed to people who were versed in the arts. Her world had always revolved around business and she'd naturally assumed that his did the same around medicine.

A pink hue overtook her cheeks as Bethany pointed out her vehicle. "The car's right over there."

He gave her his arm to hang on to. They proceeded carefully. His shoes were rubber soled and he was far more sure-footed than she was, but he took small steps to match her pace. The snow crunched beneath their feet as they went.

"Is it true?" he asked, breaking the silence just as they reached her sedan.

She wasn't sure what he was asking about. "That it's my car?"

They'd reached their intended destination, but he was in no hurry to reclaim his arm. He rather liked the way she held on to it. "That you've always depended on the kindness of strangers."

Maybe that had been giving too much of herself away, even though it had sounded like a flippant remark. "Well, I've moved around a bit, so most of the people I interact with are strangers."

Which brought up another question in his mind. "Why did you move around so much? Army brat?"

The question made her laugh. Her father in a uniform, now there was an image. "Hardly. Both my parents made their mark in the corporate world." Nannies had raised her and her older sister because her parents put in ten-, twelve-hour days, seduced by the promise of success, then working even harder once it came. "For the most part, I lived in New York until I went away to college."

"And afterward?"

"Afterward, I moved around."

"Which brings us back to why?" He looked into her eyes. "Unless you think it's none of my business."

It wasn't, but she answered him anyway. "I was looking for the right fit," she replied, and then asked a question of her own. "Is this part of some psychological workup, Dr. Wilder?"

He shook his head. "Not my department." And then he looked down into her eyes. "We've kissed in the snow, Bethany. I think we can dispense with the formalities, don't you?"

She shrugged, looking away. The parking lot had thinned out a great deal. What was left had a layer of snow on it. "I guess maybe we can. Does this mean you're going to use my first name when you growl at me at the next meeting?"

"I didn't growl," he protested. "I just raised my voice a little."

She smirked at him.

Peter blew out a breath. She was right, he'd let his anger get the better of him. "If I growled, I apologize. For the sound, not the sentiment," he emphasized, wanting to be honest with her.

Bethany inclined her head. They'd made a little progress, she supposed. "Fair enough. Does this mean that you're willing to listen to the positive side of NHC taking over the hospital?"

She asked the question with a smile

that he found very difficult to resist. He supposed that he could listen. That didn't mean she could convince him, because some things were written in stone. But to refuse to listen made him out to be irrationally stubborn and he didn't want her thinking of him that way. Not after what had just happened between them.

"I might be willing to listen," he allowed, enunciating each word.

"But?" she pressed, sensing that the word was hovering about, waiting to emerge from his lips.

"No 'but,'" he assured her. "Just a condition."

"A condition," she echoed. "What condition?"

She was looking at him warily. It amused him. No one had ever thought of him as someone to be wary of. "If you let me buy you a cup of coffee, I let you talk."

He expected her to be relieved, and perhaps a little embarrassed for being so suspicious. She appeared to be neither.

"Is this going to be like the last time you bought me coffee? You walked out on me in mid-sentence," she reminded him when he looked at her quizzically.

"No, it won't," he said with a warm smile. "This isn't going to be like the last time. You can finish your sentence and I'll finish my coffee." He turned to his right. "There's a coffee shop two blocks down. It's open late. Is that out of your way?"

"No, it's not."

Maybe he wasn't quite the stick-in-the-mud she had thought he was. Lord knows he didn't kiss like a stick-in-the-mud. He kissed like a man who knew his way around women. But then, she didn't have much experience in that area.

Bethany smiled up at him and nodded. "Okay, you're on." She glanced over toward his car. "I can drive," she suggested. "Since your car looks like it's gone into hibernation for the winter."

"No, I think I should dig it out." The sooner he got it running again, the better. "Don't go anywhere," he cautioned.

"And miss the chance of engaging in another argument with the chief of staff?" she teased. "I think not."

He stopped. "Temporary chief of staff," he reminded her.

"You could be chief permanently if you wanted the position."

She said it with such certainty, he almost believed that she meant it. He wanted to set her straight before things got too complicated. Peter shook his head. "I don't want it."

Bethany stared at him. He wasn't being modest, she realized—he was serious. He didn't want to be chief. She couldn't understand that. Couldn't understand not wanting to advance, not being driven to strive ever further. She couldn't understand a man who wasn't goal oriented, who didn't want to climb to the top of the mountain just to claim it. Her whole life had been filled with personal challenges, with pushing herself to the next goal, the next finish line. It was all she'd ever known.

"Why not?" she asked, mystified.

The answer was simple. "Because I'm busy enough. Because being chief of staff or chairman of the board of directors or holding down any official position that has to do with the hospital, takes time away from doing what I was meant to do, what I love doing. I love being a doctor. I love helping people."

"You could help them more in a position of power," Bethany insisted. "You could dictate policy if you were the chairman."

He decided that she must have known far more influential chairmen than the one who ran the hospital's board. "No, I couldn't. I could make suggestions and have them up for a vote, during which time I would spend my time arguing with a bright up-and-coming Princeton MBA graduate."

She smiled. "And this is different from the present situation how?"

He grinned. "Well, right now I have more time to devote to my patients than I would if I were tangled up in all the paperwork and demands on my time that either position ultimately requires."

Peter saw her nod her head, whether in agreement or because she was just giving up, he didn't know. But for now, it was enough.

He turned away from her and began to walk to his vehicle. The dark blue sedan was half-submerged in snow, just as she had pointed out. Mentally, he crossed his fingers and hoped the engine would start once he turned the key in the ignition.

"Peter!" she called to him. As he turned around, he heard her yell, "Think fast!"

He didn't think fast enough.

A snowball came flying at him, hitting him in the face. He heard her laughing gleefully. Without pausing, he squatted down and scooped up a handful of snow, packing it quickly with the expertise he'd acquired living in Massachusetts and growing up with three siblings.

He let it loose, getting her on the chin.

Bethany shrieked with laughter as snow

found its way under her coat, drizzling down along her throat.

"Oh God, that's cold," she cried, shivering as she brushed away the snow.

He was already prepared to fire off another salvo, but he stopped, his arm raised behind his head. "Give up?" he challenged.

It went against her grain to give up, even when it came to something as simple as a snowball fight. But she had a feeling that pitted against him in this sort of contest, she'd lose. It was better to do it now—before she got any colder—than later.

"For now," she conceded.

There was something in her tone alerting him that this really wasn't over. Dropping the snowball to the ground, he brushed the remnants of the snow off his overcoat.

"Does that mean I should be on my guard?"

Her eyes reflected her amusement and what he could only describe as a delighted wickedness.

"Maybe," she laughed. "Consider yourself warned, Dr. Wilder."

"Peter," he corrected.

"Peter," she echoed.

"I will," he responded. "But that warning works both ways," he added.

It gave her pause.

Without quite turning his back on her, Peter hurriedly brushed off some of the snow that had settled on top of the hood of his car before getting in. He turned the key in the ignition. The car made a futile-sounding noise, as if it were coughing, then suddenly fell stone-cold silent.

He tried again. This time there wasn't even a hint of a sound.

On his third try, the car cautiously came to life. Relieved, he let the engine run for a couple of minutes, wanting the vehicle to warm up before he took it out of park.

Waiting, he got out for a moment and called to her. "Want me to lead the way?"

"I know where it is," she assured him. "I'll lead the way."

With that, she got into her car. After a

couple of false starts, it came to life and she peeled out of the parking lot. Snow flew away from both sides of her vehicle as the tires made their way through the lot.

"Of course you will," Peter murmured under his breath. He got back in behind the wheel. Closing his door, he threw the car into Drive and took off after her.

The woman drove like she kissed, he thought. Fast and hard.

Peter pressed down hard on the accelerator. He was determined to keep up.

Chapter Eight

Peter arrived in the parking lot some five minutes after Bethany did. He'd been harnessed by such little things as obedience to speed limits and not flying through yellow lights that were turning red. Because of the hour and the weather, the tiny lot was all but empty.

Peter parked his car beside hers. When he got out, so did she. She looked rather satisfied with herself, he thought. "This wasn't a race, you know."

She had the good grace to look somewhat contrite. "Sorry, I'm always in a hurry to get where I'm going."

"I noticed that." She appeared set to dash up the two steps leading to the coffee shop door. "Hold it."

She looked at him, puzzled. Was there a lecture in the wings? "What?"

"You have snow in your hair." He brushed it aside with his fingertips. "Makes you look like an ice princess." The moment he said the words, he saw her eyes cloud. "What?" he wanted to know. "What did I say?"

"Nothing." Bethany turned away and walked up to the entrance. The snow on the shop's roof made it look almost quaint.

Moving ahead of her, Peter opened the door and held it. The warm air within the shop instantly brushed over her face, making the cold a thing of the past. She took a breath.

Silly to act that way, she upbraided herself. It had been years since she'd heard the taunting term applied to her and she knew that Wilder didn't mean it in the same way. Just an unfortunate choice of words, that's all, she thought.

The shop was empty except for one person sitting alone at a table near the front counter. About to walk over to a table, Peter curbed his impulse. Instead, he let Bethany choose one, sensing that she'd prefer it that way.

"You don't want to talk about it," he guessed.

Stopping by a table in the middle of the shop, she unbuttoned her coat and draped it over the back of the chair before sitting down. "No."

Peter followed suit, sliding into his chair after leaving his overcoat on the back. The waitress came over, an old-fashioned order pad in her hand. He found that oddly reassuring, given that orders were now electronically taken and submitted in some of the more upscale restaurants in Walnut River.

He waited until the young woman retreated before leaning across the table and responding to Bethany's answer. "Fair enough. I won't push."

She knew what he was saying. That he respected her desire not to discuss the matter while she'd continued to push for a lengthy discussion of the blessings involved in Northeastern Healthcare's possible takeover.

Well, he was wrong here, too, she thought. "Apples and oranges, Peter. One subject's personal, the other is very, very public."

"Patient care should be personal." His voice was mild, his feeling wasn't.

In a perfect world, he'd be right, she thought. But the world was far from perfect. They had to do the best they could and make use of every opportunity that came up. And being taken under NHC's wing was a genuine opportunity.

"It's a noble sentiment," she allowed. "But it really is no longer possible."

He nodded at the waitress as the woman returned with two cups of coffee and the

Danish he'd convinced Bethany to split between them.

"Well, it isn't if we all just give up and focus on a paycheck," he said, once the waitress had left their table again.

Bethany gave him the benefit of the doubt, since he seemed to be so impassioned about the subject. Maybe the man was too close to see the big picture. "Medicine is specialized now."

That would presuppose that what NHC offered was special and, as far as he was concerned, the HMO route detracted from medicine, it didn't add to it.

Raising his cup to his lips, he took a swallow and let the black, bitter brew wind through his system. "Working for an HMO is too compartmentalized. I don't treat a left pinkie or a right toe, I treat—"

She sighed wearily. "The whole patient, yes, I know. So you said. But in the time you've spent with that one *whole* patient, you could have helped three."

She was still thinking assembly line. That didn't work in this case. People brought nuances, shades of gray, individuality, to the table. They weren't all the same. "Or missed important symptoms for all three because I was moving so fast."

She stirred in cream and raised her eyes to his. "No, you wouldn't."

All right, he'd bite, Peter thought. "And why wouldn't I?"

"Because you're good," she said simply. "You're experienced."

Gotcha. The woman had just made his argument for him, Peter thought. "I got that experience one patient at a time."

They were going around in circles. "In your grandfather's day, doctors could do that—make house calls, be devoted to their patients like he was—"

"You've been looking into my background?" he interrupted, surprised. He hadn't mentioned that his grandfather had been a doctor.

When it became clear that he was going to be a stumbling block, she'd made it her mission to learn as much as she could about Peter Wilder. She liked to know what she was dealing with. With the possible exception of when he'd just kissed her, she really didn't like surprises. "I like being thorough—"

He was quick to feed her words back to her. "So do I, that's my point."

He was fast when he wanted to be, she'd give him that, Bethany thought. But she was just as sharp, if not sharper. "And my point is that medicine has made an awful lot of wonderful strides and breakthroughs in the last couple of decades, things your grandfather wouldn't have dreamed of."

He broke off a piece of the Danish. Glazed sugar drizzled down from his fingers just before he popped the piece into his mouth. It didn't take a clairvoyant to see where she was going with this. "And you're saying these breakthroughs wouldn't have been possible without the backing of conglomerates like NHC."

He noticed that there was a small, triumphant toss of her head accompanying the single enthusiastic word. "Exactly."

Before he could respond, she held up her hand, stopping what she knew was going to be an onslaught of information.

"I'm not saying that medicine was in the Dark Ages before managed care came along, but you have to admit that progress has definitely sped up since it came on the scene. By operating efficiently, HMOs like NHC can fund research projects, secure the latest equipment for their clinics and hospitals—"

Peter cut in, feeling that he knew a little more about that situation than she did, no matter what she professed to the contrary. "Equipment that a physician has to plead with the powers that be to use because usage is so expensive," he reminded her.

She looked down at the pastry in her fingers, uncomfortable with the fact he'd just tossed at her. She couldn't, in good conscience, tell him he was wrong. "Sometimes," she conceded.

"A lot of times," Peter countered. Placing his hand on hers, he claimed another small piece of the pastry.

Bethany drew back her hand self-consciously. "Look, I—"

He'd had enough of this confounding dance during work hours. Right now, all he wanted was to share a cup of coffee and a few unnecessary calories with a woman who, heaven help him, stirred him in a way he hadn't been stirred in a very long time.

"Bethany," he began quietly, his eyes pinning hers, "why don't we just call a truce for now and enjoy our coffee?"

Why did that make her more nervous than discussing the takeover? She tried to bank down the odd flutter in her stomach. "And talk about what? The weather?"

He laughed in response and looked out the window that faced the parking lot. It had started snowing again. "Beats being out in it."

She followed his gaze and groaned. She could feel her feet getting cold already. "Well, we'll have to be soon enough."

But right now, they were warm and dry. "Do you always take the pessimistic view of everything?"

"It's not pessimistic," she informed him, her chin raising defensively. "It's realistic."

She was an overachiever, he thought. An overachiever used to being in charge. But somewhere along the line, the woman had obviously forgotten the reason she was trying so hard. She'd gotten caught up in the race and forgotten the reason.

He studied her thoughtfully, peering at her over his coffee cup. "I bet you got straight A's in school."

Where had that come from? "Not that it has anything to do with anything, but yes, I did."

It had a lot to do with things, Peter thought. It told him the kind of person she was. Determined. Relentless. And probably very hard on herself if she fell short.

"Your parents must have been really proud."

She made a small, disparaging sound. "If they were, they never let on." She saw the interest that instantly entered his eyes and silently chastised herself. What was she thinking, letting that slip out?

"They were too busy to notice?" he asked.

She bristled at the sympathy she heard in his voice. God, but she didn't want any pity from him. She'd done just fine. Successful people didn't need pity.

"They had—have," she corrected herself, "important positions. There was a lot of demand on their time," she explained. She was making excuses for her parents, she realized. The words felt awkward in her mouth. "They were trying to give my sister and me a quality life."

Peter read between the lines. It wasn't that uncommon a story. "And they wound up skimping on the quantity, didn't they?" he guessed.

He saw her squaring her shoulders and wondered if she was conscious of the action. Was she gearing up for a fight?

"We had the best education, a beautiful penthouse apartment, everything we could ask for," she said proudly.

"Bedtime stories?"

Her mind came to a skidding halt. She

couldn't have heard him correctly. "What?"

"Bedtime stories," he repeated, breaking off yet another piece from the swiftly dwindling pastry. The portion that was left was small. He pushed the plate toward her. "Did your parents read you and your sister bedtime stories?"

"No." They were rarely home when she and her sister were young. "I didn't need bedtime stories," she informed him, then finished the last of the Danish.

"Every child needs that," he said with gentle authority.

She sighed. He was making her feel as if she had been denied something important. She didn't like being made to feel that way. "Is that what you want to do, Peter?" she asked sarcastically. "Read your patients bedtime stories?"

He smiled and shook his head. "No, I can bond without that." Taking a napkin, he wiped his fingers carefully as he regarded her with interest. "Do you see her often?"

She needed a map to keep track of this conversation. "Who?"

"Your sister."

"Belinda? No," she replied, "not often." Bethany could see that Wilder was going to push this. She nipped it in the bud. "She's living in London, has been for three years." She shrugged slightly. "Some fantastic job for an international banking firm." And their parents were proud of her, she added silently. Belinda had been the older one, the one who did things first. Anything Bethany achieved had to be bigger and better or it wouldn't be noticed.

But she'd made her peace with that, she insisted silently. *Right?*

"So your sister has an MBA, too."

"From Yale," she told him. That trumped hers from Princeton. The thought always rose in her mind when she told anyone about her sister. Needing to take out her frustrations on someone, she glared at Peter. "You make it sound as if getting an MBA is like coming down with some kind of a disease."

That wasn't his doing—she'd come up

with that all on her own, he thought. "Only if the degree robs you of your sense of humanity."

She shook her head. "Tell me, do you leave your halo and wings in your office, or do you take them home every night so you can polish them?"

The woman was working up a full head of steam, he thought. The best defense was a good offense. It was one of the rare sports analogies that he was familiar with.

The cell phone belonging to the man at the far end of the floor rang as if on cue. Peter smiled. "I think we're supposed to go back to our corners, now."

Since he'd mentioned it, this *was* a little like a boxing match. And that, she thought, was probably her fault. She doubted that he would have initiated a conversation about NHC on his own.

Not that it seemed to be getting her anywhere. She was tired and not at her best. "Why don't we table this for the night?" she suggested.

He was more than happy to accommodate her. "Fine with me. I'd rather talk about you, anyway."

They weren't going that route, either. "And I would rather go to bed." No sooner were they uttered than her words came back to her. One second before her cheeks turned an electrifying shade of pink, bordering on red.

"I mean my bed." That still sounded like an invitation, she thought, embarrassed. "Alone. To sleep," she added with an almost desperate note in her voice.

Laughing, he took pity on her and let her off the hook. "Relax, Bethany. I didn't take that to be an invitation."

She was relieved, and yet there was a small part—a very small part, she qualified—that wasn't so relieved. That was insulted.

Memories of being the butt of everyone's jokes in elementary school and junior high came rushing back to her with such a force, they all but stole her breath.

Was he being insulting? After kissing her? Or maybe *because* he'd kissed her.

"Why not?" she demanded. "Do you find me that unattractive?"

Seemingly bemused, he looked at her. "Do you even own a mirror?" he asked. "Because if you do, I suggest you look into it more often. If anyone could pull me out of my workaholic state, it would be you—" he paused "—as long as you promised not to launch into another debate in the middle of a heated embrace."

Flustered, yet at the same time warmly pleased, Bethany was at a loss as to what to say. She didn't want to encourage him, and yet, if she were being totally honest with herself, she didn't want to completely discourage him, either.

The upshot was, she didn't know what to say in response. She had no practice here, no experience to draw on. For her, flirtation, or whatever this was, constituted uncharted waters.

And then he came to her rescue. "I think we should call it a night."

She grasped the excuse with both hands. "Yes, so do I."

He smiled, pretending not to notice how relieved she looked. "We agree on something. That's a good sign. Maybe I'll bring you around yet."

She'd been so intent these past few days on getting him to change his mind and thinking of him as being incredibly stubborn, it had never occurred to her that he might be trying to change her mind, as well. This put everything in a slightly different light. Made the verbal tennis game a little trickier.

"Don't count on it," she told him.

"Counting" on it wouldn't have been the way he would have put it. Still, one thing was certain. His outlook. "Oh, but I'm an optimist, remember?"

How could he hem her in so effectively when the words were of her own choosing? "I—"

Whatever she was about to say was cut short by the sound of squealing brakes and the screech of tires. A bone-jarring crash followed, as the sound of metal twisting and entangling itself about the obstacle it had just disastrously met echoed through the coffee shop.

Peter was on his feet instantly, forgetting his overcoat behind him.

Stunned, Bethany's mouth dropped open as she watched him fly out the front door. She felt the blast of cold air from the open door.

"Peter, wait," she called. "You forgot your coat."

But the door was already shutting, separating them. Leaving her inside the warm shop while he braved the cold without any regard for himself.

Hastily throwing on her own coat, she grabbed his and hurried out the door.

The cold threw its skeletal arms around her, locking her in a frigid embrace. As the warmth of the shop swiftly faded, Bethany initially had trouble focusing.

And then she saw the accident.

She didn't have far to look. The car she'd heard screeching had crashed into a utility pole so hard, two-thirds of it had folded up into itself, forming a grotesque metal accordion. Luckily for the driver, his car had spun around and it was the rear of the vehicle that was compressed.

Had it been the front, there was no way the teenager would have survived the impact.

By the time she reached Peter, he had managed to pull the teenager free of the wreckage.

The windshield had shattered, as had one of the side windows. His attention never leaving the victim, Peter pointed that out to her.

"Call 911," he instructed.

She nodded, already pulling her cell phone from her coat pocket. "You forgot your coat." She handed Peter the garment and then quickly hit the three crucial numbers on her phone's keypad.

Someone picked up immediately.

As she spoke to the dispatcher on the other end of the line, Bethany watched Peter drape his coat over the driver in an effort to keep the teenager warm.

But not before he began ripping a strip of the lining out.

"What are you doing?" she cried.

The lining resisted but finally separated from the coat. "Trying to stop the bleeding."

"With the lining from your overcoat?" she asked incredulously.

"It's not the most hygienic way to go," he agreed, "but it's all I've got unless I use my shirt." Even as he wrapped the material around the young man's arm, he could feel Bethany staring at him. "What?" he finally asked.

"Did it ever occur to you that if something goes wrong, this guy you're working over might just turn around and sue you? And if he doesn't, maybe his parents will?"

Peter shook his head. He couldn't think about things like that now. It wasn't the way he operated. "Frankly, no," he admitted freely. "I have people like you for that."

Chapter Nine

The police and paramedics arrived less than ten minutes after Bethany had placed the 911 call. The sounds of their approaching sirens created a chilling cacophony of noise.

Peter gave as much information as he could to both the paramedics and the fresh-faced officer who looked as if he was only minutes out of the academy. In the case of the latter, Peter began by saying that he didn't really have much to offer. He hadn't witnessed the accident and he wasn't acquainted with the victim, who was still unconscious. The officer clearly wished he had more information.

The paramedic appeared pleased with not only Peter's recitation of vital signs, but what he had done while waiting for the ambulance to arrive. Bethany realized that the two knew each other by the way the paramedic spoke.

"Nice work, Doc. If you hadn't been here to stop the bleeding, we'd be taking this kid down to the morgue instead of to the hospital." As carefully as possible, he and his partner transferred the teenager from the ground to the gurney they'd taken from the back of the ambulance.

Stepping out of their way, Peter brushed away the compliment. At this point in his career, saving lives was second nature to him.

He nodded back toward the parking lot. "I'll get my car and follow you in," he said to the lead paramedic, then bent over to retrieve his bloodstained and rumpled overcoat.

"See you there," the paramedic told Peter just before he closed and secured the rear doors of the ambulance. Walking to the front of the vehicle, he opened the driver's side and got into the cab.

Bethany looked at Peter. "You're going back to the hospital?"

Peter brushed off as much snow as he could before putting his overcoat back on. She sounded surprised, he thought, trying to gauge her tone. "Yes."

She wanted to dissuade him. His hours were over. The man wasn't a robot. "Whoever's on call at the E.R. can take care of him."

It didn't matter who was on call. The teenager had become his patient the moment he'd applied the makeshift bandage to his wound. "I started this, I might as well finish it."

He actually meant that. He was willing to give up his evening, his free time, for a stranger. She looked at him for a long moment. Everything he'd said before wasn't just lip service or arguing for argument's sake. Though she tried not to be, Bethany had to admit she was impressed.

"You really are as dedicated as they say, aren't you?"

He shrugged. "I have no idea what *they* say." He didn't do things based on what someone else might or might not say or think. He did things because they were the right things to do. "So I can't answer that." To his surprise, instead of saying anything, Bethany placed herself in front of him, blocking his path to his car, and began unbuttoning his overcoat. What was this all about? "What are you doing?"

"You mis-buttoned your coat," she said, beginning to rebutton the overcoat correctly. "Not that putting the right button into the right hole really matters. You still look like a homeless person," she declared. Stepping back, she shook her head. His coat was a mess. "You're not going to be able to get that blood out."

Peter glanced down at his coat. She was

probably right. "Small price to pay for saving a man's life," he commented.

She tried to picture her father saying that with any kind of true feeling and couldn't. Her parents had a completely different set of sensibilities than Wilder obviously did. And there was something almost hypnotically fascinating about his world.

About him.

The unbidden, fleeting thought jarred Bethany right down to the roots of her teeth.

Maybe hypothermia was setting in and she was hallucinating. She really wasn't sure of anything anymore. Especially not since he'd kissed her.

Peter paused for a moment. "You'll be okay going home?" Because if she felt uneasy for some reason, then he'd follow her home before going to the hospital.

What a strange question, she thought. The man was a roving, card-carrying knight in shining armor.

"I have been up to now," she assured him. She had no idea why she added, "So I guess the cup of coffee is over."

He'd begun to walk to his car and stopped to look at her. A strange pang nipped at his stomach. Peter realized that he didn't want it to be over. But of course it was, and after all, it had only been a cup of coffee, not an actual date. Not even a preliminary meeting to set up a date.

But it could have been.

And then an impulse burst over him. "That fund-raiser Henry's throwing together, the one to raise money for the new MRI machine…"

Bethany bristled slightly. Wilder made the reference as if she wouldn't be aware of what the fund-raiser was for without his sidebar. He didn't think much of her, did he? As the efficiency expert, she was very aware of everything that was going on in the hospital. Maybe even more aware of things than he was. She was in the business of knowing everything about the hospital's operation.

"What about it?" she asked formally.

"Are you going?"

Why? Didn't he think she'd attend a fund-raiser? "Yes."

He almost stopped, thinking it wiser to keep his next question to himself. But that same impulse he'd had a moment ago experienced a fresh surge and he heard himself ask, "With anyone?"

"No." That was the honest answer. The next moment, she backtracked. "I mean—" This was where she pulled a name out of a hat to cover herself. To make it seem that she wasn't the social loner she actually was. Why she felt her lips moving and heard her voice repeating "No," she had no idea. The only answer seemed to be that she was turning on herself.

Caught up in her own unraveling, she certainly didn't expect to hear him say the next words.

"If you're not going with anyone, would you mind if I took you?"

Stunned, she recovered fast. "No, I wouldn't mind." Bethany felt her mouth curving in response. "Are you asking me out, Dr. Wilder—um, Peter?"

He grinned. "I guess I am."

Say yes. What've you got to lose? She took a deep breath. "All right."

"All right?" he echoed quizzically. He didn't know if she was agreeing with what he'd just said, or if she was agreeing to go to the fund-raiser with him. This woman, above all others, should have come with a set of instructions or some kind of manual.

"All right," she repeated. "I'll go to this fund-raiser with you. Since we're both going," she added. After a slight pause, she added more. "We can economize and use one car. Less gas—"

His eyes met hers. "Bethany."

His eyes seemed to pin her in place. She stopped in mid-sentence. "What?"

He smiled at her. "You don't have to justify your decision to me."

"I'm not," she said. Lowering her eyes, she addressed her shoes. "I'm justifying it to me."

"Oh." Turning the key, he started his car.

It instantly hummed to life. "I'll see you in the morning."

She nodded, rooted to the spot, watching him drive away. Was that a throwaway phrase he'd just uttered, or was he planning on actually seeing her tomorrow? Except for the board meetings and when she deliberately went out of her way to look for him, they didn't see each other ordinarily.

Her body was tingling when she turned away, whether from the cold or anticipation, she couldn't decide. She was hoping for the former.

Turning away, she went to her own car a few steps away. She knew what she needed—to make her mind a blank, to think about nothing and no one.

That wasn't the easiest thing to do, especially not after he'd kissed her.

He'd kissed her.

The thought vividly brought back the sensation. Instantly, she became warm. So much so that for a moment, she simply sat in her car, frozen in the moment. Enjoying the moment.

And then she became disgusted with herself. She was pathetic, Bethany silently chided. Most women her age fantasized about the lovers they'd had; they didn't go on and on about a single kiss no matter how good, how toe-curling it was.

Enough!

Bethany started up her car and headed toward the residential development where she lived. What she needed, she told herself, was some hot soup and a diverting program on TV.

That's not what you need, a soft voice whispered in her head.

Maybe not, she countered, banking her thoughts down before they got any more out of hand. But hot soup and TV was what she was going to get.

Peter walked into his house and turned on the light. He stomped his feet on the small scatter rug just inside the threshold, trying to knock as much snow as possible off his shoes.

It had been a long evening. He'd put in

another two hours at the E.R., but the teenager, Matthew Sayers, was going to be all right. His parents had all but flown to the hospital the second the police had called them about their son's car accident. Both had expressed overwhelming gratitude to Peter for coming to Matthew's aid and for "saving our boy," as Matthew's mother had sobbed.

It turned out that the Sayers were quite well-to-do. Matthew's father was a top-level magazine executive and his mother was an heiress. They had only recently bought their house in Walnut River. They also owned a condo in Manhattan. The senior Sayers wanted to show his appreciation for having his son tended to.

After being enthusiastically pressed several times, Peter had finally made a suggestion to the man, which was how Walnut River General got its first donation toward the MRI machine.

A sense of satisfaction pervaded him.

All in all, it had been a very productive evening. He'd saved a boy and gotten

Henry a sizable donation to kick-start the fund-raiser.

He'd also kissed an angel.

The stray thought made him smile. Memory of the kiss had been moved temporarily to the back of the line because of the urgent situation he'd had to deal with, but now it had reappeared at the front, swiftly growing in proportion.

Despite the time that had lapsed, he could still taste her on his lips. Still taste the subtle flavor of ripened strawberries.

The overhead light dimmed for a second, then returned full strength.

Probably the work of the storm, he thought. Outside, the wind was howling and the snow was falling harder. Perfect conditions for a power outage. It wouldn't hurt to keep a flashlight handy, he decided. Just in case.

He kept a couple of flashlights on the bottom shelf of his anemically stocked pantry. Shrugging out of his overcoat, he left it draped over the first piece of furniture he came to—the sofa.

Bethany was right, he thought, glancing at the coat. It looked like something a homeless man would wear. One particularly down on his luck. He was going to have to see about buying another one. He certainly didn't want the woman to be embarrassed to be seen with him.

The thought that had just floated through his head bemused him. When, other than at the gala, would that be happening? And why would her feelings about his appearance even come into play? Assuming she *had* any feelings about his appearance.

His thoughts were definitely going in strange, uncharted directions. Peter pushed the question and its accompanying thoughts away. He had no desire to get emotionally involved with anyone again. He was too weary and too wired at the same time to properly tackle anything right now.

As he walked through the room to reach the kitchen, his eyes were drawn to the envelope that was still lying on the mantelpiece. The envelope with his father's handwriting on it.

The one he still hadn't opened.

Haven't had the time, Peter thought defensively.

Was that it? Was a lack of time the reason he hadn't opened the envelope, or was it really more of a lack of nerve? Was he afraid of what he might read, what he might discover?

He shook off the thought.

This was ridiculous. He was a grown man, a doctor for God's sake. He'd had his hand inside a patient's stomach, dealing with a perforated ulcer, had to face a grieving wife to give her the gut-wrenching news that her husband was gone. Had had to summon the courage to step, at least partially, into his father's shoes. Those kinds of actions weren't the actions of a man who lacked nerve.

So why was an envelope causing perspiration to pop out all over his brow?

What was it that he was afraid of?

And then he knew. He was afraid of finding out that rather than a saint, his father had just been a man. Fallible.

Ridiculous. Stop stalling, Wilder.

With determination, Peter walked into his kitchen. Crossing to the pantry, he opened it. The flashlights were just where he'd left them, on the bottom shelf. The pantry contained very little else. A box of matches, a collection of napkins in the corner. Containers of salt, pepper and sugar and one opened box of stale cereal.

Taking the larger of the two flashlights, he checked to see if it worked—it did—and then walked back into the living room. To confront the monster hiding in the closet.

Or lying on the mantelpiece, as it were.

Peter set the flashlight facedown on the mantel and picked up the envelope. After taking a deep breath and then letting it out, he ripped open the envelope. His fingers felt ever so slightly icy.

Inside the envelope was a letter and another, thinner envelope. This one was addressed to Anna.

Was this some kind of a game? Like the little gaily painted wooden Russian dolls, the ones where when you opened one up, exposed another, smaller doll inside, and then another, and another until there were six or more lined up, each one smaller than the last?

Were there other envelopes, addressed to David and Ella, inside this one? Was this some strange inside joke from the grave?

There was only one way to find out.

Bracing himself even as he silently argued that there was no reason to feel this kind of apprehension, Peter decided it might be prudent to sit down before he began to read.

He perched rather than sat on the sofa, tension taking less than subtle possession of his body. The air felt almost brittle as he drew it in.

The letter was handwritten, and reading was slow going. While not illegible, his father's handwriting was a challenge at times.

"To my son Peter,

From the first moment you drew breath, I have always thought of you as my successor. Not just at the hospital, but with the family as well. I am very proud of the man that you have become. You are so much more than I ever was or could hope to be."

Peter frowned. What did *that* mean? An uneasiness continued to build within him. He forced himself to continue reading.

"I don't want to burden you with this. But you are the only one I can ask to make this decision. You are the only one I can trust with this secret.

By now you've noticed that there is a second letter, addressed to Anna. I am leaving it up to you to decide whether or not she would be better off knowing. Knowing what, you may ask. Or perhaps, since you were always so bright, so intuitive, you already know. Your mother always suspected but never asked. I think she was afraid of the truth.

Anna is not your adopted sister, she is your half sister. Her mother was an E.R. nurse who was very kind to me during that period when your mother and I were having such a difficult time together. You were nine at the time so perhaps you don't remember. Your mother had been suffering from depression, and had retreated to her own world. A world she later emerged from, thank God. But while it was happening, it was terrible for both of us.

I had my work, and you boys, but I felt lost and, in a moment of weakness, I gave in and accepted the comfort of another woman. Anna is the result of that single liaison. Her mother, Monica, knew she wasn't going to be able to raise her and give her the things she would need to succeed in this life so she gave her up.

We agreed that she would leave the baby on the steps of the hospital and that I would "find" her there.

Not long afterward, Monica died in a plane crash. I've debated taking this secret to my grave, but part of me felt that Anna should know the truth. That she was always my daughter—and your sibling—in every way. However, if you think that she would be better off not knowing, then burn this letter, and hers as well.

Please don't think any less of me because of my transgression. I am still your father and I love each of you—and your late mother—very much.

Forgive me,

Your loving father, James."

Peter sat, holding the letter in his hands and staring at it, his mind completely numb, for a very long time.

Chapter Ten

Peter wasn't sure exactly how long he sat there. When he finally managed to rouse himself, he felt the bitter taste of betrayal in his mouth as he slowly tucked the letter and the other envelope back inside the original one.

Taking a breath, he could feel, awakening inside him, a whole host of emotions warring with one another. Most prominent of all was disappointment, mixed with confusion.

He wished he'd never read the letter, had never been given this burden to deal with.

Never been robbed.

Because that was what it was—robbery, pure and simple. His father's confession had robbed him of the image that, until this evening, he had carried around with him.

Yes, he knew the man was not a saint, that he was flesh and blood and human, capable of making mistakes. But he'd always assumed that those mistakes would be tied in with judgment calls about his patients. Maybe an occasional failure to diagnose a particularly elusive illness properly.

Never in his wildest dreams would he have believed that his father would be guilty of personal misconduct. He would have gone so far as to swear on a stack of Bibles that his father had never strayed, never cheated on his mother, never been anything but loyal and faithful to everyone he knew, especially to the people in his immediate family.

Instead, James Wilder had betrayed his wife and, in a way, Anna.

No—all of them, Peter thought, trying in vain to bank down the hurt he felt.

This showed him another side to his father, a far more human side than he was willing to cope with at the moment. If his father had done something like this, had hidden a secret of this magnitude, were there other secrets that James Wilder *hadn't* admitted to?

Here he was, trying to preserve his father's legacy and maybe it was all just a huge sham, illusions created by smoke and mirrors to hide the actual man.

Maybe he really didn't know his father at all.

Who knew, maybe his father would have jumped at the opportunity to have the hospital taken over by an HMO, to have someone pocket all the expenses, pay for everything and ultimately remove the responsibility for judgment calls from his hands.

Maybe…

No. Discovering that his father had had a relationship—and a child—with another woman while married to his mother, didn't change the things that mattered. The basic things. And it sure as hell didn't change the man that *he* was, Peter thought angrily.

He hadn't based his feelings, his position, on the fact that his father would have done it this way. That his father would have approved of the stand he was taking. Believing that had only served as reinforcement. He, Dr. Peter Wilder, *believed* in what he'd said to Bethany and to the board. Believed that, when it came to the hospital, the old ways *were* the best and that Walnut River General would be much better off *not* being swallowed up whole by a soulless, unemotional con-glomerate, no matter *what* kind of promises were made.

Rising to his feet, he sighed heavily and shook his head. He felt drained and ex-hausted beyond words.

Peter put the envelope back on the man-telpiece, not wanting to touch it any more right now. Wishing he could wipe its existence from his mind. But he wouldn't be able to do that, even if he threw his letter and Anna's into the fire.

"I wish you hadn't told me this, Dad. I wish you hadn't passed the burden on to me," he whispered, aching.

Everything fell into place now. It all made sense to him.

This was why his father always seemed to go out of his way for Anna, treat her differently, share more time with her than he did with the rest of them. It wasn't because he was trying to make up for her feeling like an outsider. He was doing it because he'd felt guilty about her very existence. Guiltier still because he didn't tell her she was his real daughter. He had let her go on thinking she'd been abandoned when just the reverse was true. She could have been put up for adoption. Instead, he'd taken her into his family rather than let her go to someone else's—and have the secret go with her.

His first instinct was to preserve his

father's memory for the others. Because this didn't just affect Anna, but David and Ella as well. It was a package deal. If he passed this letter on to Anna, once she read it, the others needed to know, too. They needed to know that the family dynamics had changed.

No, Peter thought as he walked up the stairs to his bedroom, that was for Anna to decide. If he told her, it would be her secret to share or keep.

He laughed shortly. Who would have ever thought that he would be aligning himself with Anna against his brother and sister?

An ironic smile curved his mouth. That wasn't altogether right now, was it? Anna was his sister, too.

His sister. His *real* sister.

Well, that explained why she seemed to have his father's eyes. Because they *were* his father's eyes.

Just when he thought there were no surprises left, he mused, shaking his head sadly.

The letter was no longer on his mantelpiece.

Early this morning, he'd gotten up and

decided to leave the thick envelope in his study, in the middle drawer of his desk until he decided what to do with it.

Meanwhile, he was still a doctor with patients, still the chief of staff, albeit temporarily, faced with a supreme dilemma: how to make the rest of the board of directors vote his way regarding the NHC takeover.

Because all options needed to be explored, someone from the grasping conglomerate would be coming at the end of the month to look them over. Supposedly to observe how they functioned, but in likelihood, to attempt to sway them with promises.

If he came out staunchly opposed to the NHC executive's visit, it would seem to the board that he was afraid of the challenge or the potential changes. Afraid that Walnut River General couldn't withstand an in-depth comparison to the way hospitals beneath NHC's massive banner were run.

He had too much on his mind to deal with the burden of his father's request right now.

But the discovery hung over him heavily and made him far more serious than usual. A couple of his patients remarked on it, as did Eva, his nurse. All of them attributed the change in mood to his father's passing.

He said nothing to correct them. This was *not* something he wanted to discuss even if he were free to do so.

The morning went on endlessly until the last patient was finally gone at twelve-thirty. It had taken Eva less than two minutes to grab her purse and run off to lunch.

"Want me to bring you back anything?" she offered just before she slipped out.

"No, I'm fine. I brought lunch." It was a lie, but his appetite had deserted him last night, making no reappearance this morning. Food was the last thing on his mind.

"Okay, I'll be back soon," she promised, exiting.

He heard the outer office door close and turned his attention back to the work he'd spread out on his desk. There were several files he wanted to review before signing off on them.

Something else he probably wouldn't be able to do soon if NHC came in, he thought. They were pushing for paperless offices. All the files would be on computer, on some nebulous server located in the middle of the country.

And what would everyone do if there was a power spike? Or a blackout. What then? What would happen to all the information that was stored?

Give me paper any day, he thought, opening the first folder he came to.

Forcing himself to focus, he was immersed in the file—and the patient—within seconds.

Preoccupied, he didn't hear the knock on his inner office door, and was startled a bit when Bethany walked in. He sighed inwardly. Any other time he'd have been glad to see her. Now, the last thing he needed was another frontal assault about the virtues of NHC.

He felt his temper shortening already. "I'm in the middle of something," he told her, then looked back at what he'd been reading.

"I won't take up much of your time," she promised. "I just came to give you this."

Curious, he looked up in time to see her place a bottle of wine, tied with a bright red ribbon, on his desk.

He eyed it for a long moment. He was familiar enough with wine to know that this was not an inexpensive bottle hastily purchased at the nearest supermarket. This brand took a bit of hunting.

Why was she bringing it to him? She couldn't possibly be trying to bribe him. Or could she? He leaned back. His eyes never left her face. "What's this?"

This was not easy for her. But she had always prided herself on being fair. "An apology."

That was the last thing he'd expected

from her. Especially since he wasn't quite sure what she was referring to. "For?"

She took a breath before answering. This was going to be a little tricky, but he'd impressed her a great deal last night. "For thinking that you're an arrogant jerk who doesn't see past his own ego."

Instead of taking offense, he laughed. At least she was being honest and, after the surprise he'd received, being honest was a very good thing. "I thought you said you thought I was a saint."

She felt relieved that he was taking this in the spirit it was intended. "No, I said *other* people thought you were a saint. To be honest, I thought that maybe you were using that image to make people see things your way."

He supposed he could understand her feeling that way, especially considering the world she came from. Big-business dealings were hardly ever without some kind of backroom dealings.

"And now you've suddenly changed your mind about me because—"

She knotted her hands before her. "Because I watched you in action. Because you didn't stop to worry about being sued if something went wrong." Even though she had deliberately pointed it out to him last night. "Because you just got in there and helped that boy simply because he was a human being in trouble." She had to admit, if only to herself, that she'd felt a certain thrill watching him rush to the rescue like some modern-day hero. "You almost make me yearn for the 'good old days.'"

He laughed, shaking his head. "You're much too young to have been around for the good old days." He said it as if he were far more than merely nine years older than she. Peter indicated the bottle of wine. "Apology accepted." Taking it in hand, he held the bottle out to her, implying that she was free to take it back. "But you really don't have to do this."

She made no move to accept the wine.

It was clear she was disappointed that he seemed not to want the peace offering.

"We don't seem to agree on anything, do we?"

Not wanting to offend her, Peter put the bottle down again. "Well, I do remember us being in agreement at one point last night." He looked at her significantly, a hint of a smile on his lips.

Bethany could feel heat rising in her cheeks.

"Perhaps one," she allowed.

"Maybe there's more where that came from," he speculated. Then, in case she thought he was suggesting something a little more personal, he added, "Agreements, I mean."

Her eyes met his. "Maybe," she echoed softly. She wasn't talking about being in agreement, only in concert. She could feel her face growing yet warmer. So much for poise. Bethany cleared her throat. "I'd better get out of your way."

"You're not in my way," he said. And suddenly, as much as he had wanted to be alone before, he didn't anymore. His father's revelation had left him in a strange, vulnerable place. He'd always felt so sure about everything, so confident. Now he wasn't. It was as if he was back in college again, just after Lisa had abruptly left him. "Stay for a minute," he urged. "Unless there's somewhere else you need to be."

He gave her a way out, but she didn't want to take it, not just yet. So she edged back toward his desk and sat down in the chair opposite his desk. "Aren't you busy?" she asked, nodding at the files.

"It's nothing that won't keep." He closed the top folder but left it where it was. "Just paperwork I thought I'd catch up on. It's a losing battle," he added with a slight, disparaging sigh. "There never seems to be enough time to catch up on it all. Besides, no one ever died saying 'I wish I'd had the chance to catch up on all my paperwork.'"

"What *would* they regret?" What would *he* regret, she couldn't help wondering.

"Not spending enough time smelling the roses." It was something he sincerely advocated but hardly ever did. The closest he came was to urge his patients to do it. "Or take in the beauty that's around them." He was looking directly at her as he said it. Her cheeks began to take on color again. "You're growing pinker," he commented, amused.

She'd give anything for a good, solid tan right now, but given the weather, it would have been rust, not tan. "The room is warm," Bethany murmured. She lowered her eyes. "If that compliment was intended for me, Peter, you might think about having your eyes checked."

This wasn't false modesty, he realized. She really meant what she was saying. "Hasn't anyone ever told you that you're beautiful before?"

Not once, she thought. Not ever. And when she was growing up, the exact opposite was true. Kids were cruel and her parents didn't provide a haven for her where she could lick her wounds. Looking back, she supposed that was a toughening device on its own.

Since he was obviously waiting for an answer, she told him the truth. "You'd be the first."

He couldn't believe that. "Where did you grow up, in a swamp covered with mud?"

The sincerity in his voice delighted her. "No, just with people who had twenty-twenty vision." Her parents, especially her mother, could be trusted to point out her flaws, but never comment on any of her attributes. They expected her to be a high achiever. Anything less was not acceptable. And there was always Belinda to live up to. "Unlike yours." A self-deprecating smile played on her lips. "I was the original ugly duckling."

"You remember the rest of the story, don't you?" he asked. "That so-called ugly duckling became a beautiful swan."

She shrugged, looking away. "I haven't reached that part yet."

If asked, he would have said that

Bethany Holloway did not lack confidence, but obviously, he would have been wrong. "Not only have you reached it, Bethany, you've surpassed it."

When she looked at him, there was something enigmatic in his expression. "What?"

Peter was silent for a long moment, debating whether or not to say anything or just shrug away her question. But she'd taken the first step and held her hand out in a truce. He couldn't be any less of a man than she was.

The second he'd thought it, he realized that it was a sexist thought, but he hadn't meant it that way. "It's my turn to offer you an apology."

"For what?" Was he apologizing for walking out on her in the cafeteria, or something else?

"For thinking you were like someone else I once knew." Maybe that was why he'd reacted so strongly against her when she put forth her arguments. "You're not a thing like her."

"Like who?" she asked. "And why do

you think would I be insulted if I'd known you were comparing us?"

"Lisa Dandridge." He saw the next question in her eyes. "Someone I once knew in college. Someone who didn't turn out to be who I thought she was. At first glance, you look a lot like her."

There were things he wasn't saying. Before she got carried away, reading between the lines, she decided to get it straight from the horse's mouth. "This Lisa, was she important to you?"

"For a while, yes." For a while, she was the moon and the stars to him. Until he'd suffered an eclipse.

"How important?" she pressed.

Well, he'd started this. He had no one to blame but himself for her question. To withdraw now wouldn't be fair. "Engaged-to-be-married important."

Bethany fell silent for a second. She hadn't expected him to say that. "Oh." There was no follow-up from him. "Well, don't leave me hanging," she prompted. "What happened?"

"We got unengaged."

She hadn't gotten to where she was by being a shrinking violet. "And that happened because…?"

Because. It was an all-purpose word that covered so much territory. "Because she found someone else."

Her mouth dropped open. "She cheated on you?" How could any woman in her right mind cheat on someone who looked like Peter? Who was obviously as decent as he was? There was no doubt in her mind that he was better off without this Lisa person.

He'd never known whether Lisa had slept with Steven Wilson, the medical student she'd left him for. He never wanted to let his thoughts go that far. It was enough that she'd left him for the reasons she'd cited.

He shrugged, looking out the window. More snow. Just what they needed, he thought. "We never got into that."

"Then why did you two break up?" He struck her as the type of man who didn't easily give up on a woman he professed to love.

Her question brought the past vividly back to him. "The 'other man' had 'more potential' than I had. He was going into his father's prestigious practice in New York and I was coming back here, to work with *my* father in a place that was far less lucrative and upscale. Lisa didn't see herself living in Walnut River. She saw herself shopping on Fifth Avenue."

"What an awful woman." The words just came out before she could stop them.

"No, Lisa just knew her limitations. Knew what would make her happy. And obviously, it wasn't going to be me."

Bethany frowned. "Well, you were better off without someone like that." She paused, thinking. "And you think I look like her?"

Peter laughed softly. "At first glance, perhaps. But you're far more beautiful than she ever was."

Bethany felt her breath backing up in her lungs. "Really?" she whispered.

"Really."

He was looking at her lips. She felt herself getting warm again. "I think I'd better get back to my office," she murmured.

He nodded. "Maybe you'd better do that," he agreed. Before he went with the demands inside him that were beginning to grow insistent. "And thanks for the wine. I'll save it until I have something to celebrate." He looked at her as she edged her way to the door. "Maybe we'll even share it together."

He was referring to the board's vote regarding the possible takeover. Did he think because she'd brought him a peace offering that she was throwing her vote in with his? Or was that his way of saying he might reconsider his own stand?

She didn't want to ask and risk spoiling the moment. So she inclined her head in agreement. "Maybe we will," she agreed as she slipped out.

He found himself smiling as he returned to his files.

Chapter Eleven

Though she told herself she wasn't, the truth of it was Bethany was looking forward to the fund-raiser. However, none of the reasons she'd cited to herself regarding why it was important to attend the function were responsible for creating that warm, nervous feeling in the pit of her stomach. There was only one reason for that.

She was going with the man who had literally made the world fade away when he'd kissed her.

Okay, so he'd kissed her and she'd liked it. *Really* liked it. But there was no reason, she told herself, to believe anything of that nature was going to happen again. It was an aberration, a once-in-a-lifetime occurrence. Peter Wilder was a healer, not a lover, even though he had a lethal mouth that had melted her like drawn butter.

Professional, she silently insisted—it was all going to be strictly professional. If there was anything she was, it was professional.

She was still silently clinging to this belief, repeating it over and over again like some kind of mantra, as she went shopping for "the right dress."

It turned out to be a gown, a gown like no other she'd ever owned. The moment she saw it on the alabaster mannequin, she'd fallen in love with the gleaming creation.

Because the gown wasn't her.

It was the kind of gown that belonged on a socialite, a jet-setter, someone who was accustomed to frequenting parties on both coasts and collecting heady, over-the-top compliments.

Depending on the light, the gown, suspended on two thin gossamerlike straps, was either silver or gray-blue, and when she put it on, it adhered to every curve she had. Moreover, it somehow miraculously awarded her more cleavage than she was accustomed to having and the material swayed provocatively with every step she took. Simultaneously, the material played peekaboo with the slit that ran from her ankle to halfway up her thigh, drawing the beholder's attention to the fact that whatever other attributes she might possess, Bethany Holloway, former card-carrying ugly duckling, had stunning, killer legs that seemed to go on forever.

Because she was ordinarily governed by more than her share of logic, Bethany put the gown back on the rack three separate times before she finally snatched it up and fairly trotted to the register.

In most cases, the purchase price of the designer gown would have been prohibitive for someone earning the kind of salary she did. But money had never been a problem for Bethany, never the bottom line that proved to be a deciding factor. What her family lacked in warmth and nurturing attributes it made up for with money. Specifically, a trust fund that was passed on through her mother's family. Martha Royce, her mother's mother, had been obscenely wealthy. The woman believed in giving her descendents a sizable jumpstart in life, not out of any sort of affection but because she believed her lineage was better than anyone else's and should be rewarded for that.

Her grandmother died the year before Bethany graduated from college. At the funeral, which included both her parents and Belinda, she was the only one who shed any tears at the woman's passing.

As she looked at herself now in her wardrobe mirror, Bethany couldn't help wondering what her grandmother would have said if she'd seen her in this gown.

You go, girl.

Bethany smiled to herself, pressing her hand to her unsettled stomach. If the stories she'd heard about the woman's youth, mostly through relatives other than her parents, were true, Grandmother had been a rebel and a hell-raiser. She only wished she had inherited a little more of the woman's spirit instead of her money.

Then, at the very least, she wouldn't feel as nervous as she did about wearing this gown.

Really, darling, this kind of a gown should be worn by someone who can carry it off, don't you think?

This time it was her mother's voice that had popped into her head to haunt her. Her mother who, even when she was seemingly praising her always made Bethany feel as if she were lacking.

Bethany set her jaw, deliberately shutting her mother's perpetually condescending voice out. She really liked the gown, liked the way she looked in it. She looked, she thought, like someone special.

She fervently hoped she wasn't just deluding herself.

The doorbell rang, breaking into her

thoughts. The next second, she could feel her stomach seizing up and her heart beginning to race.

Maybe this was a mistake. What was she trying to prove? This backless, almost strapless silvery revelry wasn't her. She belonged in subdued colors, quiet shades that didn't call attention to all the things she lacked. Her nerves spiked to incredible highs as she looked toward her closet.

But it was too late to change, too late to surrender to second thoughts on their third pass-through. She was going to have to wear this.

Here goes nothing.

Taking a deep breath, Bethany walked out of her bedroom and to the front door on legs she willed to be steady.

Opening the door, she summoned her brightest, most carefree smile—or some reasonable facsimile thereof.

And then she saw him. Peter was wearing a formal tux. God, but he looked handsome.

"Hi," she heard herself murmur through lips that felt frozen in place.

The next moment, she saw Peter's dark eyes slowly travel down the length of her before returning to her face. Unable to tell what he was thinking, she held her breath, waiting for the verdict.

He already knew, even if she professed not to, that Bethany was beautiful. But in this dress, she transcended anything that had come before. The word *vision* didn't even begin to cover it, but it was the only word his numbed brain would come up with.

Realizing that he was staring, Peter cleared his throat. He was stalling, searching for his voice. There was a very real danger of it emerging in a squeak. She did take his breath away.

When he smiled, she could feel warmth spreading all through her.

"I should have brought my portable defibulator," he murmured. When she raised a quizzical eyebrow, he explained, "I think my heart just stopped."

Was he teasing her? Telling her it was inappropriate? Rather than become defensive, she bowed to his experience. This was her first fund-raiser at Walnut River General and she didn't want to look out of place.

Bethany looked down at her dress. "You think it's too much?"

He laughed at the innocent question. "On the contrary, I don't think it's enough." He saw the uneasiness enter her eyes and quickly added, "I mean, it's fine with me, but I'm not sure I'm up on my dueling techniques."

"Dueling techniques?" she repeated, confused.

He nodded. "The way I see it, I might be called upon several times this evening to defend your honor."

He *was* teasing, but in a nice way. Pleasure whispered through her.

Bethany caught her lower lip between her teeth in an unselfconscious, endearing way that just further evaporated his breath. At this rate, he was going to need an oxygen tank before they reached the hotel ballroom.

"I could change," she offered.

He didn't see that as an option. She was almost too beautiful to bear. "And break the hearts of every single male over the age of eight within ten miles? I think not."

So what was he telling her? That he liked the way she looked? Or was he trying to say something else? Bemused, she shook her head. "You certainly know how to confuse a girl with a compliment."

He couldn't help but laugh at the word she'd used. He would have thought that the term "girl" would have offended her. She was more reasonable than he'd given her credit for. He liked that.

"Trust me, Bethany," he assured her. "You might still feel like a girl inside, but outside, you are all woman."

She felt her cheeks warming. This was getting to be a habit around him. She tried to divert his attention from the deepening hue of her skin. "When did you learn to be so charming?"

"About two minutes ago, when you opened the door."

It wasn't the answer she was expecting. He definitely wasn't the stiff, humorless man she'd initially taken him for. Bethany picked up her coat and her purse from the sofa where she'd placed them earlier. "You really are full of surprises, aren't you?"

Peter took the long black coat out of her hands and helped her into it. "The same can be said of you. Those two-piece business suits you wear at the hospital don't begin to adequately convey what's beneath."

She tried her best not to glow at the compliment, but it wasn't easy. "Nice to see you out of a lab coat, too." Turning around, she looked at him again. His overcoat was open, giving her a full view of the tuxedo he wore. She noticed something else, as well. "You look younger."

"That could be because tonight, I don't have the weight of the world on my shoulders." With his hand at the small of her back, he escorted her out the door. Bethany paused to lock her door. Turning, she took hold of his arm before she realized what she was doing. It just seemed like the natural thing to do. He smiled, completing his thought. "Just a beautiful woman on my arm."

The cold wind carried the scent of another impending snowfall, whipping around, chilling any exposed area it could find.

"About that vision test…" she began playfully as she took small, careful steps to the curb where he had parked his vehicle.

"You should schedule to have one immediately," he agreed. "You're obviously not seeing how beautiful you really are."

Blushing, she slid into the passenger seat and waited for him to round the hood and get in on his side. When he did, she said, "Uncle."

Seat belt in his hand, he stopped midmotion and looked at her quizzically. "Excuse me?"

"Isn't that what you cry when you know you're outmatched?" Bethany asked. She vaguely remembered hearing that once. "Uncle?"

Peter turned the key in the ignition. After a second, the car started up. He was going to have to remember to check his antifreeze level, he told himself. "Yes, but why—"

She sat back in her seat as they pulled out of the driveway. "I didn't think that such a person existed, but you can clearly outtalk me."

He spared Bethany a glance and smiled at her warmly. "Nice to know."

Just as he'd expected, everyone in the ballroom turned their way when they walked in. Bethany looked far too stunning tonight for people to nonchalantly absorb her into the group without first appreciating every sensual inch of her.

The first to approach them, with the other members of the board not to far behind, was the chairman. The expression on Wallace's moonlike face was that of extreme pride, as if he'd had a hand in inventing Bethany.

Wallace hadn't even been the one to hire

her. That had been his father's doing, in order to get the hospital to run more smoothly, Peter thought. At least he could thank his father for something.

An odd sensation undulated through him. It took Peter several moments before he recognized it for what it was: possessiveness.

What was that all about? he demanded silently.

This was just a casual date. No commitments involved. There was nothing for him to feel possessive about.

Yet there it was, this feeling nibbling away at him, leaving tiny grooves in its wake.

As if to prove to himself that this was absurd, that he felt no such attachment, Peter began to step back. To his surprise, Bethany tightened her hold on his arm, forcing him to remain where he was.

This was a new turn of events, he thought. A couple of weeks ago, she would have been relieved to have him go.

"Would you like something to eat?" He

leaned forward, whispering the question in her ear.

It was only through the greatest control that Bethany managed to stifle the shiver that shimmied up and down her bare spine in response to the feel of his breath along the side of her neck.

"That would be very nice," she murmured. Any second now, her heart was going to pound right out of her chest.

He continued to linger, to draw in the subtle scent of perfume in her hair and along her skin. "Anything in particular you'd like?

She turned to face him. "Surprise me."

Damn but he'd like to. He'd probably surprise all of them if he gave in and did what he wanted to: whisk her out of here and back to his house.

Back to his bed.

Lord, when was the last time that he'd even thought like this? Like some knuckle-dragging Neanderthal?

Like a man who longed for a woman?

Peter inclined his head. "All right," he promised.

He really did need to start socializing more, Peter thought as he made his way over to the buffet table that ran along one wall.

The affair was being catered by a company that was doing it all at cost. It was their donation to the institution that had long treated most members of the owner's family.

Ella was standing at the far end of the table, contemplating her choices. Despite the clusters of people scattered along the perimeter doing the same thing, for all intents and purposes, Ella appeared to be alone.

Since their father's death, she'd withdrawn into herself, working at the hospital and then slipping home, spending most of her time alone. Though he would have never pushed her toward it, Peter was glad she'd decided to attend the fund-raiser.

Taking a plate, he queued up behind her. "How are you doing, kiddo?" he asked quietly.

Preoccupied, Ella seemed a little

startled as she turned around to look at him. "Oh, Peter, hi." His question played itself back in her head. "I'm fine," she replied, keeping her voice light. "I had a slightly tricky procedure today, but I think I handled myself well. It turned out all right in the end. Patient's doing very well…"

"I don't mean professionally," Peter said, cutting in. He deliberately looked down into her eyes. "How are *you* doing?"

Ella's shrug was vague and, for a moment, she looked away. She knew what he was asking. Taking the protective covering from her wounds was difficult. But this was Peter, so she forced herself to do it. Because he'd asked.

"It's hard for me to believe that I'm not going to run into him somewhere in the hospital. That Dad's not going to come walking around the corner at any minute." She sighed, making choices from the buffet without really paying attention to the canapés she placed on her plate. "He was bigger than life, you know?"

A few days ago, it would have taken no effort on his part to agree with her because he'd shared that opinion. But now…now it took a bit of doing for him to keep the truth from surfacing. It took effort to nod his head and say, "Yes, I know what you mean."

Another sigh escaped her lips and she nodded, as if in response to something she'd hypothesized in her mind. "I guess it's going to take time before things are back to normal for us."

Here he couldn't flatly agree. Wouldn't be able to face himself in the mirror come morning if he didn't contradict her, because nothing was ever going to be the same again. Not for him. Not for the rest of them if he decided to share the secret.

But this was Ella and his instinctive need to protect her had him tempering his response. "I doubt," he told her slowly, "that things are going to get back to normal anytime soon."

Because the hospital staff was all speculating about the possible takeover by NHC, Ella thought he was talking about that. She knew how he felt about it without having to ask.

Ella placed her hand on his and squeezed, offering comfort. He seemed surprised. "Don't worry, Peter. Northeastern Healthcare isn't going to come and gobble us up."

It was on the tip of his tongue to say he wasn't referring to that, but then he stopped. It was better this way, better for her to think he was preoccupied about the takeover and not what he'd learned about their father. "What makes you so sure?"

She flashed what he'd always referred to as her thousand-watt smile. "Because we have the great Dr. Peter Wilder fighting our fight for us," she told him with affection, patting his cheek. "And you're not going to let anything happen to Dad's hospital."

Right now, he couldn't bring himself to think of the hospital in those terms. "The hospital belongs to all of us—and to the town."

"Right," she agreed. "And that's the way

Dad saw it, but I still can't help thinking of it as his baby."

"Whether he meant to or not." The words had just slipped out.

She stared at him, confused. "Excuse me?"

Damn, he was going to have to exercise better control over himself than that, Peter silently chided. "Sorry, my mind wandered for a moment."

The light of understanding entered her eyes as Ella looked over her shoulder toward Bethany and the circle formed by some of the other board members who were attempting to engage her in conversation.

"I can't blame you," Ella said. "She is really a knockout." And then her gaze returned to her brother. She regarded him with unabashed curiosity. "Are the two of you, you know, involved?"

That was all he needed, for a rumor to get started. He didn't want that pushing them together. He was already having enough trouble standing on level ground.

"Only in keeping Walnut River General an excellent hospital," he answered. "The problem is, we have two very different opinions on how that might be accomplished."

"So I've heard." And then she smiled. "Well, if anyone can change her mind, Peter, it'll be you."

She was giving him far too much credit, he thought. "I'm not a knight in shining armor, Ella."

"Next best thing—a doctor in a brilliant white lab coat." Ella paused to kiss her big brother's cheek. "Don't ever stop being who you are, Peter. I couldn't stand it if you suddenly changed."

And how, he wondered, would Ella take the news that her beloved father had changed from an angel to a man with feet of clay? Or, at the very least, that he'd had one fall from grace and then compounded it a thousandfold by never owning up to the truth?

Again he felt the weight of his father's secret all but bending his back. At that moment, he found himself resenting his father.

"Whoops," Ella declared, looking toward a far-off corner of the room, "there's Ben Crawford. I've been trying to get a hold of him all day for a consult. Excuse me, Peter, but I've got to corner him before he gets away again." And with that, she made her way across the ballroom.

"You look pensive," Bethany said, coming up beside him. "Ella all right?" And then she added, "You were taking your time with the food and I thought it might be easier if I came to get my own."

"Right." He handed her a plate, feeling slightly guilty that he'd forgotten all about bringing her back something to eat the way he'd promised. Talking to Ella had steered his thoughts in another direction. "Ella's doing as well as can be expected."

She picked up two stuffed mushrooms, placing them side by side on her plate. "You two seem to have a good relationship. I was watching," she confessed. "You're lucky. Both of you."

The way she said it had him reading between the lines again. "You don't have a good relationship with your sister?"

"I don't have any relationship at all," she admitted. It wasn't something she was proud of. "We competed as children. After college, we went our separate ways. It's been more than a year since we spoke."

He recalled that she'd mentioned her sister worked at a bank in England. "They don't have telephones in England?"

"Yes." She put two tiny popovers onto her plate. "And she doesn't call."

The woman was too bright to miss the obvious, he thought. But he said it anyway. "Last I checked, phone lines worked both ways. Sometimes all it takes to start the healing process is taking the first step."

It would take more than that, she thought. "You moonlight as an advice columnist?"

He laughed, then deposited a couple more canapés on her plate before taking some for himself. "All part of being a doctor."

He meant that. Not for the first time she thought to herself that Peter Wilder was really a very rare man. And, not for the first time, she felt an accompanying little flutter in the pit of her stomach as she thought it. Except that the flutter was getting bigger each time. She was going to have to watch that.

Chapter Twelve

Observing people had always been a hobby for Peter. At a very young age, he'd discovered he could tell a lot by the way people interacted with one another. For the most part, people fascinated him.

But tonight, watching the different board members cluster around Bethany—not to mention studying more than a handful of the male physicians buzzing around her like so many bees who had lost their navigational system—caused a mild irritation to rise up within him. Irritation, and—he conceded—perhaps a minor case of jealousy as well. He didn't like it. He'd always believed that jealousy was a useless, demeaning emotion.

So why did he feel like separating Bethany from her admiring throng and keeping her all to himself?

Where the hell were all these primitive feelings coming from? Moreover, where were they going to lead him? He wasn't all that certain he wanted to know.

When the orchestra began to play after dinner, Peter decided that maybe it was time to stop trying to figure out what was going on internally and just make the most of the moment.

Coming up behind her chair, Peter bent down until his lips were next to her ear and asked, "Would you care to dance?"

Bethany abruptly ended her conversation with the neurologist who had been monopolizing her for the past ten minutes and looked at Peter quizzically. She seemed surprised. "You dance?"

He inclined his head in silent assent. "That would be what my question implies, yes."

Bethany had trouble wrapping her mind around the concept. She thought of Peter as intelligent, capable, generous and kind. Fluid and graceful, however, did not enter the picture.

"Funny," she said, rising. "I never thought of you as someone who would enjoy dancing."

"How *did* you think of me?" Taking her hand, he led her to the dance floor. "Besides the obvious." When he turned to face her, he smiled, prodding her memory. "I believe you said something about my being a stick-in-the-mud?"

Bethany's smile was rueful. "I was wrong," she admitted freely. Then, as anticipation flared within her veins, she added in a quieter voice, "About a lot of things."

Taking her hand, he tucked it against his shoulder, then placed his other hand at the small of her back. His palm came in contact with her bare skin. He'd forgotten that there was no material there. Desire shot out to the foreground.

"Such as?" he prodded gently after a beat.

They were swaying to the music, their bodies all but merging. All sorts of feelings were swarming inside of her, feelings that hadn't visited before— except perhaps since he'd kissed her.

She found herself aching for a repeat performance. Aching for a great many things. Everyone around them began to fade away.

Raising her head, Bethany looked up into his eyes. "Some things are better left unsaid."

"I can appreciate boundaries," he told her indulgently.

Until just now, he'd thought that his own were fairly well defined and in place. But now, suddenly, they felt as if they were crumbling. Holding her to him like this, feeling the heat of her body mingling with his, he could feel those barriers shattering like so much glass being struck by a stone. When she leaned her head on his shoulder, her hair brushing against his chin, he could feel everything within him tightening as heat traveled up and down his body, making him aware of every single inch of hers.

As they continued to dance, he tried not to breathe in the scent of her hair, tried not to let his mind wander down paths that would ultimately lead nowhere, but his thoughts refused to be bridled.

When the musicians stopped playing, Peter and Bethany were still dancing, their bodies moving in time to a melody all their own.

Bethany laughed, then covered her mouth to lock in the sound. It was late and all the lights of the houses that surrounded hers were off. The neighborhood was asleep.

It might be asleep, but she felt wide-awake. Wide-awake and ready to go. Anticipation pulsed all through her like a horse at the starting gate.

"We could buy two MRI machines with the money that was raised tonight," she declared.

Peter had driven her home and she was

now vainly searching for her keys in a purse that should have given her no trouble because of its minute size. She still couldn't locate them.

"I had no idea there were that many well-off people in Walnut River. Walnut River," she repeated. Another infectious laugh, quieter this time, escaped. "That sounds like a quaint town that should be down the road from *Little House On The Prairie*." She looked at him to see if he agreed, then went back to swishing her fingers around the bottom of her purse, seeking to come in contact with metal.

"Henry knows a lot of people." Amusement curved his lips as he watched her rummage. The lady, he thought, had had a few too many. Uninhibited, she was adorable. "People who like to feel good about themselves because they give to good causes. By the way, that was a sizable donation you offered," he pointed out. She'd made the pledge after having her second or third glass of wine. She was new at this sort of thing, he judged. People who didn't ordinarily drink tended to be a little reckless when they did imbibe. "At the risk of being indelicate—"

Her head shot up. Was that hope in her eyes? Couldn't be.

"Yes?"

He didn't want to see her embarrassed when it came time to make good on the pledges. "Can you actually afford it?"

God, but he was proper. She'd thought he was about to say something a lot more personal, a lot more intimate, than ask about her financial state.

"Sure. I'm rich." And it had been more of a burden than a boon most of the time, she thought sadly. "Didn't you know that? Got a trust fund and everything. But it's a secret." To underscore the point, Bethany placed her forefinger to her lips, as if to seal in the sound of her words.

He wasn't quite following her and wondered if the wine was jumbling up her thoughts. "Your trust fund's a secret?"

Still searching through her purse, she nodded. "Don't want anyone to know,"

Bethany said, then sighed. "People don't believe you're serious about your work if they know you're well-off. They think you're just slumming, amusing yourself," she announced, saying it as if it was the latest cause that needed to be taken up. And then her eyes brightened. "Ah, here it is."

Triumphantly, she pulled the key ring from her purse and held it up.

Getting said key into the lock proved to be yet another challenge. Bethany missed the opening twice, hitting the door instead. On her third attempt, she dropped the key ring altogether.

She looked down at the keys as if they'd escaped. "Oops."

Peter bent down and retrieved her key chain. Rather than hand it to her, he decided it would be simpler if he just unlocked her door, so he did. Turning the knob, he opened the door, pushing it so that she could walk in first.

He followed her into the house, then placed the key on the small table next to the door. She swayed a little as she turned around to face him. He caught her by the shoulders to steady her. "I think you had a little too much wine."

Unfazed, she looked up at him and said, "I did."

She made it sound as if she'd done it on purpose. He couldn't fathom her reasoning. "Why?"

She took a heartening breath before answering. "Because if I hadn't, I wouldn't be able to do this."

"This" turned out to be wrapping her arms around his neck and sealing both her lips and her body to his as if her very life depended on it.

Caught off guard, Peter's initial reaction was to tighten his arms around Bethany's waist, kissing her back with as much fervor as she was exuding.

An urgency traveled through his body, making demands he knew he couldn't, in all good conscience, follow through on.

So after allowing himself a heady, breathless moment, he summoned a surge of strength—not exactly as easily as he would have liked—and placed his hands on the inviting swell of her hips. Rather than give in and mold her to him the way he really wanted to, Peter gently pushed her back, away from him.

Bethany blinked, dazed, surprised and bewildered. Why had he stopped? "What's wrong?"

The innocent question squeezed his heart. "Nothing." He tried to make her understand his reason for backing away, wishing that either she was clearheaded or he had no conscience. But neither was true. "Bethany, you're tipsy."

Her smile was quick, sinking him like a stone. "We've already established that." But as she tried to drape her arms around his neck again, he stopped her. His hands on hers, he lightly disengaged her hold. "What?" she cried. Didn't he want her?

Peter shook his head. This nobility was killing him. "I can't take advantage of you like this."

"You're not taking advantage," she

pointed out, frustrated. "You're just standing still. I'm the one taking advantage." Standing on her toes, she laced her fingers together behind his head. "So stop giving me an argument and let me do it, damn it."

He laughed. He'd always sensed she was aggressive, but not in this vein. It would take so little to give in, to stop trying to talk her out of it and just enjoy what was happening. It had been a long time since he'd been with a woman and she was the first one who had aroused him in eons. It felt as if there was lighting in his veins.

"Bethany," he protested, knowing he had to protect her from herself, "this isn't you."

"Well, it should be," she insisted, pouting so adorably he was sorely tempted to nibble on the lower lip she stuck out. "The sober Bethany is repressed. She's afraid to feel anything because once she opens up those doors, she knows she can also feel pain. Feel the hurt when others talk about her." She lowered her eyes and he thought he saw tears shimmering in them. "Feel inadequate because she's always falling short."

She got to him. The sad look in her eyes, the heartwrenching downward twist of her mouth, it all got to him. Slipping one arm around her shoulders, Peter lightly ran the back of his hand along her cheek, her mouth.

"There's nothing for you to feel inadequate about, Bethany," he told her softly.

"Then why won't you kiss me?" she cried. "Don't you want to?"

So badly that it hurts. "You have no idea how much I want to."

"Then why won't you do it?"

He could feel her breath along his skin, could feel himself capitulating even as he struggled to hold on to his control.

"Because if I kiss you, it won't stop there." He moved a soft curl back from her forehead. "And I don't want you waking up tomorrow morning, regretting what you did."

"I won't," she insisted.

He almost believed her. Almost. He'd never known what temptation meant until this very moment. "You have no way of knowing that. You're not in any position to make that kind of decision."

She shook her head, feathering her fingers through his hair. Shaking up his soul. "You sound like me. Weighing, measuring, debating and, ultimately, doing nothing." She turned up her face to his, imploring him to not turn away from her. "I don't want to be that way anymore. I want to ring the bell, reach for the stars." She took a breath and said it. "I want you to make love with me."

Did she have any idea what she was doing to him? "Bethany…"

A smile moved the corners of her mouth. "Unless, of course, you're some kind of alien and this is going to lead to your secret identity being uncovered."

Where did she get this kind of stuff? Serious one second, adorably silly the next? He was losing ground and he couldn't hold out much longer, noble thoughts or no noble thoughts. "I'm not an alien."

She nodded her head a bit too hard. "Good, because I wouldn't have been up for that."

"You're not up for this, either." He was going to have to carry her up the stairs, he thought. She just wasn't steady on her feet. "Go on to bed, Bethany. You'll thank me in the morning."

Rather than turn toward the staircase, Bethany latched onto his lapels and yanked, drawing him down closer to her level.

"Only if you're in the bed with me," she breathed. And then, before he had the opportunity to say anything else, to turn her down again, Bethany raised her mouth to his.

She caught his lower lip between her teeth and ran her tongue along it. When she heard the low moan escape, she knew she'd won.

Peter knew he damn well should have been stronger than this. He wasn't one of those men who went from conquest to conquest, thinking of sex as the greatest indoor sport ever invented. He *had* no love life to speak of and, other than an occasional moment of loneliness, he was fine with the path he'd chosen.

But this was different. *She* was different and, try as he might to resist her, he couldn't help himself.

There'd been electricity humming between them, possibly from the first moment they'd stood on opposite sides of the takeover. He liked the way her eyes flashed when she talked and the way every fiber of her being seemed to be brought into the argument, even if he ultimately did disagree with her.

Her passion stirred him then and it was certainly doing a number on him now. Any reserve he thought he had went completely out the proverbial window.

Especially when he felt her hands tugging his jacket off his arms, her fingers fumbling with the buttons on his shirt.

In comparison to her, he was wearing much too much in the way of clothing.

Still kissing her, he began helping

Bethany remove the various cloth barriers that kept her soft, tempting flesh from his. Shucking out of his trousers, flinging off his shirt and the cummerbund that made his attire so formal.

His body thrilled to her touch, to the feel of her fingers against his skin. It was with great self control that he refrained from working her free of the shimmering gown until the very end.

It was the prize at the end of the rainbow.

She had no idea where this frenzy was coming from. It was as if something inside of her, something that had been waiting patiently and quietly to be set free had just taken over.

When he pressed his lips to the hollow of her throat, she moaned, her knees all but buckling. The next moment, she felt the shadow-thin straps of her gown being coaxed in unison from her shoulders. Within a heartbeat, the gown had left her breasts, sinking seductively to her waist. Instead of material, his hands covered her, igniting a fire within.

Bethany kissed him over and over again, unable to get enough, afraid to stop because she was afraid that she might disintegrate into a million little pieces if she did.

Her breath seemed to back up in her lungs as Peter slid the gown from her hips, leaving her standing only in the whisper of a thong she'd bought this afternoon, a last-minute purchase to go with her gown.

Bethany felt the urgency of his body as it hardened against hers. And then suddenly she was airborne. Peter lifted her into his arms and brought her over to the sofa, carrying her as if she were some precious treasure he'd been entrusted with.

His lips whispered along her body, warming her, generating huge waves of desire, leaving her begging for more.

Over and over again he kissed her, with feeling, with restraint, with fervor, all the while continuing to melt her.

When his mouth just barely grazed the

skin along her belly, Bethany felt everything within her quickening. Felt desire take her prisoner, demanding things she'd never experienced before.

He made her head spin, her blood rush in her veins and her breath all but evaporate. She twisted and turned beneath his hands as they caressed and explored, beneath his warm mouth as he drew the woman she wanted to be to the surface.

His tongue teased, aroused and nearly drove her over the edge.

It was agony. It was ecstasy. And she desperately wanted more, wanted to be his in every conceivable way possible.

Never in her wildest dreams had she thought it could ever, *ever*, be this wonderful, being with a man. Making love with a man.

Bethany was arching against him, tearing the last shreds of restraint out of his fingers. He'd wanted her from the moment she'd kissed him. It had been only through the greatest effort that he held back, determined to pleasure her, to make as sure as he was able that she wouldn't regret this in a few hours.

Working his way up along her slender body, he paused for a moment as he pivoted above her, just looking at her face. He had been so certain that he'd never feel the kind of desire that would bring him to this point, would never want a woman this much again, and yet, here he was, a smoldering cauldron of emotions and feelings.

Bringing his mouth down to hers, Peter moved her legs apart with his knee and thrust his hips forward, trying to move slowly.

Bethany locked her arms around his neck and pulled him closer, and Peter was helpless to resist. Desire flamed, stronger than ever. He drove himself into her, taking what she offered so urgently.

Chapter Thirteen

Bethany had never felt such peace, never been quite as happy, as she was during those precious moments in Peter's arms.

The heavy breathing slowed and became regular, both his and hers. She was aware of Peter shifting his weight, moving off her until he lay beside her. Aware, too, of the silence that was becoming all-pervasive and almost deafening.

She could only interpret it one way. She felt sadness elbowing its way in.

She had to ask.

"Disappointed?"

As she uttered the word, Bethany struggled to steel herself for what she felt was the inevitable answer. Refusing to look his way, to see the answer, or worse, pity, in his face, in his eyes, she stared at the ceiling instead.

Her question seemed to come out of nowhere and it caught him off guard. He took a minute to think about his answer.

"With myself? Yes. With you?" he guessed when she didn't say anything. He turned to look at her quizzically. How could she possibly even think that? "How could I be?"

She ran her tongue along her lips. They felt as dry as dust, not to mention that her throat felt as if it was constricting.

She didn't believe him.

All her inadequacies, all the criticisms she'd endured through her adolescence, came flying back to her. How could she have been so stupid as to think he could feel something for her? That he could enjoy himself a fraction as much as she had. What had possessed her to push so hard? If there had been something between them, something to be nurtured, she'd just destroyed it.

He was looking at her, she could feel it, waiting for her to answer. Bethany forced the words out. They scraped along her dried lips. "Because I'm not exactly all that experienced."

She heard him laugh softly to himself. Was he laughing at her? Oh God, she couldn't stand that. "There's such a thing as a born natural, Bethany," he finally said. "*You,*" he emphasized, "fall into that category."

"You don't have to be nice." Although she was grateful for it, she thought. The very tight knot in her stomach loosened just a little.

He raised himself up on his elbow to look down at her. The thought that there hadn't been a parade of men through her life pleased him. "*Nice* has nothing to do with it," he assured her. "I'm being truthful."

Her eyes slanted toward him, and then, summoning her courage, she slowly turned her face to him as well. "Then it was all right? You enjoyed yourself?" she asked in a hesitant, low whisper.

He ran his hand lightly along her cheek, wondering what sort of things were going on in her head. Could a woman as beautiful, as poised as she was really be plagued by such insecurities?

"Despite the fact that I just did a terrible thing, yes," he said, "I did. And *enjoy* is a very small, inadequate word in this case."

She took heart in his second sentence, but it was his first one that confused her. "What terrible thing?"

"Made love with you even though you weren't thinking clearly and even though you were…" His voice trailed off for a moment, looking for a delicate enough way to say what he wanted to say without having her feel insecure all over again.

"Tipsy?" she supplied.

Peter nodded. "A man and a woman's first time together should be special."

She turned so that her body brushed up against his. Her eyes were large, luminous. They peered into him, drawing him in all over again.

"What makes you think it wasn't?" she breathed.

He touched her face. "I think there's something between us, Bethany. If I hadn't made love to you here tonight, it would have happened in the not-too-distant-future." He smiled at her, truly sorry for what he'd robbed her of. "It would have been a night for you to remember."

Placing her hands on his chest, she leaned her head on them and raised her eyes to his face. Again, she asked, "What makes you think it isn't?"

Cupping the back of her head, Peter brought her down to him and kissed her mouth.

Within moments, the lyrical dance began all over again, this time in a slower, richer tempo. This time, Peter felt he was making love with a woman he was certain wanted exactly the same thing he did. Guilt was no longer an uninvited guest at the proceedings.

Dawn hadn't yet arrived when music suddenly splintered the stillness and Bethany's rhythmic breathing.

Beethoven's *Fifth Symphony*?

Where was *that* coming from?

Prying her eyes open, trying to make sense of the sound which was half in her dream, half in her waking consciousness, Bethany heard the music stop, replaced by a voice.

A male voice.

In her bedroom.

Her thought process imploded, collapsing completely in on itself and demanding to be restructured. Now.

Stunned surprise gave way to memories. Last night came flooding back to her in vivid color and wide-screen. With a start, she bolted upright, then belatedly grabbed the sheet that had pooled around her waist. She yanked it back up to where it could do some good.

Peter was sitting up, talking on the phone. His back was to her.

They were in her bedroom, in her bed, and it was obvious that they had both fallen asleep after they'd made love that third time.

The fog left her brain just in time for her to hear Peter say, "I'll be right there."

Holding the sheet, she drew her knees up to her chest and dragged her hand through her hair. Wishing she could drag her brain into place as easily.

She cleared her throat, doing her best to sound as if everything was normal when right now, everything was anything *but*.

"Be right where?" she echoed.

Shutting the cell phone that had awakened her, Peter placed it back on the nightstand and shifted around in order to look at her. "The hospital."

"The hospital?" she repeated as if saying what he said would somehow clear everything up for her. But it didn't. "You're going to the hospital at—" she looked at the clock on her side of the bed "—four-thirty in the morning?"

"Emergencies don't happen on schedule," he said lightly.

God, but he didn't want to leave her. She looked incredibly enticing with sleep still whispering along her eyes. His hand swept along her throat, tilting her head back a little. He allowed himself only a moment to brush his lips over hers.

This could become an intoxicating habit, he caught himself thinking.

"I was going to make you breakfast, but I'm afraid I'm going to have to give you a rain check, instead."

"You cook?" she asked in disbelief. She barely knew how not to burn water.

He got out of bed and quickly slipped on his underwear and trousers, then put on his shirt. There would be amused comments about his formal attire at the hospital, but he could handle that.

"Cook, dance, I can actually sew on a button in a pinch," he told her, "but I don't like admitting that."

He looked at her just before he began buttoning up his shirt. His fingers froze in place. The sheet was molded to her, but his imagination was vivid enough to do away with the barrier and remember her as she'd been last night. Fluid. Golden. And all his.

The shirt remained hanging open as he leaned over the bed to kiss her one last time. "And, just in case there are any doubts still lingering this morning, you were magnificent," he assured her.

Breaking away, he made it all the way to the door before he impulsively retraced his steps to the bed and swept her into his arms to kiss her one last—last time.

He sighed as he drew his head back. "You know, this is going to make it very hard to argue in the boardroom," he surmised. "I'll keep picturing you just the way you are right now."

Bethany blushed. "I know," she whispered, agreeing with his first statement. Arguing—debating about *anything*—was the furthest thing from her mind right now.

She could feel her body aching, her hunger returning. She knew it was selfish, but she didn't want him to go. "Are you sure that emergency has your name on it?"

Her very tone was coaxing him to remain. But he had to resist. He had his oath to honor. "'Fraid so. The patient's wife specifically asked for me when they brought him in."

"Oh." She'd learned that he had legions of patients, people who swore by him and didn't want to have anyone else touch them. She could understand that. If she had something wrong, she'd want him to be her doctor.

With a sigh, she gave up her claim to him. For now. "Then I guess you'd better ride to the rescue." She gathered the sheet around her again. "How long do you think it'll take?"

He shook his head. There was no way he could tell right now. It wasn't like an oil change on a car. "I don't even know what's wrong yet."

Wearing the sheet like a toga, trying

not to trip on the hem, she followed him to the doorway. "Will you come back after you're finished?"

He didn't want her curtailing her schedule and waiting, especially when he didn't know when he'd be finished. "Depends on the time."

That wasn't what she wanted to hear. But rather than retreat, she made a bid for his time. "It shouldn't." She waved her hand around vaguely. "It's Sunday, supposedly a day of rest. You can come back here whenever you're finished. To rest." A mischievous grin curved her mouth before entering her eyes. "Or whatever."

He looked at her, amused. "To rest?" There damn well wouldn't be any resting done and she knew it. She'd all but wiped him out as it was. He was going to need this emergency just to recharge.

"Or whatever," she repeated, her smile now positively wicked.

He liked the sound of that.

Peter laughed, shaking his head. He needed to be on his way, and yet he couldn't help lingering a second longer. It took all the resolve he had not to tug away the sheet she was clutching to her.

"I didn't know the real you, did I?" he speculated. There was so much more to her than he'd initially believed.

"Neither did I," she confessed. She stepped back, allowing him to cross the threshold. To leave her. "Hurry," she urged as he turned away.

"As fast as I'm able," he promised.

And still do a good job. That part he'd left unsaid, but having come to know the man the way she did in these past few weeks, Bethany knew that was what he meant. The man probably was incapable of doing anything less than his best.

She had no idea where the sense of pride that suddenly washed over her came from. After all, the man really wasn't hers. There was no joint bond between them, nothing to suggest that his triumphs were also hers by proxy. And yet she knew that if someone said something positive about him, she'd be the one to feel the pride. Probably more than he.

With a sigh, rather than abandon the sheet and face the day, she made her way back to bed and got in. She could almost, if she tried very hard, still feel the warmth on his side of the bed.

For a second, she splayed her hand out, absorbing it. She closed her eyes, envisioning him still there. But that led her nowhere.

Holding her knees close to her, wrapping her arms around them, she stared off into the darkness, thinking of Peter.

She was dressed and all the things that had wound up scattered over the floor last night had been picked up, cleaned up and put back in their rightful places by the time Peter finally returned to her house later that day. It was just past one in the afternoon and he had been gone a full eight hours.

The moment he rang the bell, she flew to the door, opening it before the last chimes faded away.

He could probably see that she'd rushed

to the door, she thought. So much for playing hard-to-get.

"I'd pretty much given up hope," she confessed as she stepped back, holding the door open wide.

She banked down a very strong urge to throw her arms around his neck and lose herself in a soul-melting kiss. No point in frightening the man off.

That was how it was done, right? If she behaved as if they belonged together, as if he was the half of her soul that had always been missing, she'd scare him off. The guy would most likely be on the first flight out of town, destination: anyplace but here.

So she went back to restraint, something that had always governed her actions up until last night.

"I had to wait for the lab results to come back," he told her. Damn, but she looked good enough to eat. "And there's only a skeleton crew on Sundays."

"People aren't supposed to be sick on a Sunday," she said lightly. "I think it's a law that's written down somewhere."

"Too bad Gerald Muffet hadn't read that particular law," he said, referring to the man who he'd been ministering to since he'd left her bed.

His tone was weary and he looked a little tired. She didn't know how to interpret that. Had he come back out of a sense of obligation, because he'd said he would? Or was he here because he really wanted to be?

She fell back on what she knew. "Did you have breakfast?" There were waffles in the freezer and a toaster on the counter. She could manage that.

When she moved like that, reaching for the toaster and bringing it closer, he could see her breasts straining against the thin white blouse she had on. He stopped being tired.

"Coffee and something out of the vending machine," he recalled vaguely, then shrugged, trying hard not to stare at her. "I don't know what."

"Sounds delicious," she said, glancing at her watch. "It's too late for brunch. Would you settle for plain old lunch?"

That wasn't the appetite that had surfaced the moment he'd begun to walk up the driveway. Certainly not the one that was ricocheting through him right now. But he didn't want her thinking of him as some rutting pig preoccupied with sex.

"Plain old lunch sounds wonderful," he assured Bethany.

She took the freshly sliced roast beef she'd dashed out to get earlier and placed it on the counter. "So what was the big emergency that couldn't be handled without dragging you out of bed?" Rolls joined the deli meat, as did a jar of mayonnaise, romaine lettuce and a green pepper.

"Man came into Walnut River General looking like death after being confined to Hilldale Memorial in the next town for almost two weeks."

She cut four slices of pepper, wrapped up the rest and returned it to the refrigerator, then sliced the rolls. "Was he a transfer?"

Sometimes a hospital would send one of their patients to Walnut River, but that was admittedly rare.

He frowned. Just thinking about it made him angry. "No, actually, they gave him a clean bill of health and sent him home, saying it was all in his head."

She deposited meat on the cut rolls and turned to look at him. "And was it?"

Peter shook his head. "Turned out to be all in his belly." Breaking off a tiny piece of the pepper, he munched on it as he watched her work. And let his mind take over. "Man had a bleeding ulcer and he'd lost approximately forty percent of his blood before he ever got to us. If his wife hadn't nagged him into coming to Walnut River General, he would have been dead by tomorrow. Probably sooner."

"I guess then in this case—" she grinned "—nagging served a purpose." Depositing a leaf of lettuce on top of the mayonnaise-slathered roast beef, she paused, playing back the facts he'd given her. "How could that other hospital have missed the fact that the man's blood supply was down by forty percent?"

He couldn't resist saying, "They were probably trying to be cost effective and skimped on the tests." Couldn't resist, because it was the truth. "Either that, or their lab tech made a mistake. It has been known to happen—far more than we'd like," he added, wishing it could be otherwise.

She put the top of the bun on top of each opened sandwich and then cut both sandwiches in half. "How did they happen to come in asking for the great Dr. Peter Wilder?" she teased.

He paused for a second, wanting to get the order right. "His wife's sister's husband is a patient of mine."

The man has a fan base, she thought with a grin. "Six degrees of separation, huh?"

He took that literally. "More like four, but in the end, all that matters is that the guy came to Walnut River and that we found the problem. With any luck, he will probably be on his way home by Tuesday."

"That's great, Peter," she said.

He'd used the word *we* but he was the one who had spearheaded everything and they both knew it. Modest on top of good. Not to mention damn sexy. Hell of a combination, she thought.

After all these years of being alone, could she finally have gotten lucky?

Turning from the counter, she impulsively ran her hand along his chest. She could feel his heart beating a little faster in response. It spurred her on to raise herself up on her toes and kiss him.

It was meant to be just a light, passing kiss. A fond expression of affection.

But it deepened the moment contact was made. So much so that neither of them came up for air until a good two minutes later.

"So," she said, trying to sound as if every molecule in her body hadn't come apart and then resurrected itself again. "What would you like to have served with your lunch? Soup? Salad? The soup's out of a can and the salad came ready-made," she qualified in case he had any concerns that her culinary attempts might make him ill.

He didn't seem to be interested in food. "How about a side order of you?" Wrapping his arms around her again, he nibbled on her ear and sent flashes of heat dancing all through her. "Better yet," he proposed, "how about you as the main course?"

She glanced at the sandwiches on the counter. "You're not hungry?"

He didn't take his eyes off her. "Starved," he contradicted.

Her mouth began to curve as anticipation took hold. "But not for food," she guessed.

He didn't say anything at first. Instead, he grinned in response and then lifted her into his arms the way he had last night. He was picking up where he'd left off this morning.

"Not for food," he confirmed just before he lowered his mouth to hers.

Chapter Fourteen

Peter's anger toward his father was slowly dissipating. In its place was empathy. It was hard to fathom how the man, as chief of staff *and* chairman of the board, not to mention being a practicing physician, ever found even five seconds to rub together. It was a wonder the man had come home at all.

Granted, Peter himself wasn't the chairman, only a member, but even that took a chunk out of his time. And he was the acting chief of staff until a permanent one could be found. Keeping everyone happy and everything running smoothly was *really* time-consuming. He was beginning to see why, in the midst of turmoil, his father might have turned to a sympathetic ear, a kindly attitude and, in a moment of weakness, allowed one thing to lead to another.

He was walking the proverbial mile in his father's shoes and beginning to think a little differently than he had before.

Right now, those shoes, after having been confined to the E.R. for the past hour, acting as a consultant for one of the other doctors, were headed in Bethany's direction. And he couldn't suppress the eagerness he was experiencing—nor did he really want to try. This was a new feeling and he wanted to savor it, to enjoy it and make it last.

He couldn't help wondering if it had been like this for his father when he'd begun seeing Anna's mother. The excitement, the anticipation that it brought into an otherwise overburdened life. He was beginning to understand his father's action a lot better. Understand and forgive.

In addition, whenever he'd had the opportunity this past month, he'd begun to sort through his father's legal papers. There was a lot to be learned about the man there, too. All good. Still, he hadn't made up his mind what to do about the letter that had started it all. The longer he waited, the harder it would be…

He didn't want to think about that, not right now.

Preoccupied, he didn't even see Henry Weisfield until he was almost on top of the hospital administrator. Henry said his name twice before he even heard the man.

"Sorry," he apologized. "I've got a few things on my mind."

The man cocked his head, studying Peter as if he hadn't seen him before. "Is it my imagination, or is there this extra—" he gesticulated in the air, searching for the right word "—spring in young Dr. Wilder's step?"

Peter avoided Harry's inquisitive gray

eyes. "I don't know what you mean." He deliberately kept his voice as vague as possible. He also slowed his pace to practically nil. He had no intention of leading Henry to his ultimate destination.

Henry laughed to himself. "Peter, you're a wonderful doctor, a great humanitarian. If I had a ruptured appendix or had only one person to choose to be stranded with on a desert island, it would be you because you always come through." He allowed the compliments to sink in before he continued. "But with all your attributes, you do have one failing."

Henry did like to build up to things and, ordinarily, Peter didn't mind. But right now, he was in a hurry. "And that is?" Peter coaxed.

"You're a lousy actor. I would think that a man with all your burdens—" and he proceeded to enumerate them "—temporary acting chief of staff, newly appointed member to the board of directors, plus the recent passing of your father, a man you admired and respected, not to mention loved, *and* the prospect of the hospital changing hands and being absorbed into the NHC stable—"

He was about to urge Henry on to his point, but the last phrase waved red flags in front of him, the way it always did. "Not going to happen," Peter told him with feeling.

"Don't be too sure," Henry commented before finally getting back on track and to his original point. "I would think that a man with all that weighing so heavily on his shoulders wouldn't look as if he's about to break into song, or at least start whistling and clicking up his heels at any moment."

Peter tried to summon a scowl, but he couldn't. He was feeling too good. Way too good. And Bethany was the reason.

"I've been reading people longer than you've been breathing," Henry was saying. "What's changed in your life?"

There was no denying it. Henry's assessment was correct. Everything the man had just mentioned should, by all rights, make him feel as if he had the weight of the world on his shoulders. Heaven knows he was still wrestling with his conscience about whether or not to shake up Anna's world by giving her their father's letter; still coming to grips with the discovery that his father had harbored dark secrets and wasn't the plain, open, selfless man everyone believed him to be. Still struggling with how to make the board reject the takeover proposition, although that was showing promise, especially since he felt he'd opened Bethany's eyes. But somehow, everything had slipped into the shadows. Eclipsed by the feeling that was generated by being with Bethany. By sharing his nights, his bed with her these past few days.

"Only one thing I know of that can do that to a man," Henry concluded. The older man's eyes narrowed beneath his bushy eyebrows. He pushed his rimless glasses up his nose and peered more closely at him, as if he were studying a slide through a powerful microscope.

"Peter," he asked suddenly, his voice lowered in utter surprise, "are you seeing someone?"

Peter smiled to himself. Seeing someone. It was a very old-fashioned term, in keeping with what his life had been like up until now. But Lord knows that despite the fact that the feelings being with Bethany created inside of him were as old as time, he felt reborn. Not unlike a gangly adolescent on the uplifting path of his first love.

Love?

There, he'd said it. Or at least finally allowed himself to think it. And doing that shook him down to his very core. But there it was.

Love.

That's what he felt for the woman who had brought light into his darkening life. Something he never thought he'd experience again. And it made all the difference in the world to him, filled him with an optimism that he could barely contain.

Still, his common sense remained intact

and that meant, at least for now, Henry wasn't going to be privy to any of this.

So he winked and smiled and said, "A gentleman never tells, Henry."

Henry cleared his throat and fixed him with a look that might have pinned a younger, less confident man to the wall.

"On the contrary. A gentleman can *always* tell Henry." When nothing was forthcoming, Henry nudged him with his elbow. "I'd all but given up on you, you know. Everyone thinks you're married to this place." The second he said it, his small eyes widened as a realization hit him. "Is it someone here?" And then he laughed at himself. "What am I saying—of course it has to be someone here. You never go anywhere else."

Peter knew exactly what the man was trying to do and he shook his head. "Talk all you want, Henry. We're not adolescent boys, hanging around a gym locker, swapping stories."

"That we are not," Henry agreed, but not for the reasons that Peter had. Both men stepped to the side, out of the way, as several nurses walked by then, going toward the elevators. "Ever since my Mildred passed on, I haven't had a story to swap.

"So who is it?" Henry asked, not about to give up. "Not Simone," he concluded, mentioning the day-shift head nurse in the E.R. "She's got eyes for that paramedic. What's-his-name, the one who has all that really dark hair."

It amazed Peter that Henry, with all his duties and responsibilities, could still take in these extraneous details. He mentioned the first paramedic that came to mind. "Mike O'Rourke?"

Henry pointed his index finger at him, as if he'd won some sort of prize by guessing correctly. "That's the one."

Peter laughed, shaking his head. "What are you, Henry, the hospital gossip?"

Henry shrugged his thin shoulders beneath his jacket. "I just pay attention to what goes on around me."

"Right." Peter knew better. "Pay attention and pass it on. And you actually expect me to tell you my secrets?"

Henry heard what he wanted to hear. "Aha, so there is someone. And, by the way," he corrected with a small, insulted sniff, "I'd rather think of myself as the relayer of interdepartmental news, not a gossip." He uttered the label disdainfully.

It was Peter's turn to shrug. He tried not to be too obvious as he glanced at his watch.

Henry was undaunted, but, began to head for the elevators. "I'll find out soon enough, you know."

Peter was relieved they were parting company. "There's nothing to find out."

"Like I said," Henry called after him, "you're a lousy actor."

Peter merely smiled to himself as he kept walking down the corridor. That was all he had to do, admit to Henry that he was "seeing" Bethany Holloway. Henry would have the news telegraphed throughout the hospital in record time. Neither he nor Bethany needed that kind of attention.

This thing, whatever "it" was, between the two of them was still new, still fresh, still without a name to define it and he was afraid that if he examined it too closely, shed too much light on it, it would fall to pieces, unable to sustain itself beneath the attention. It needed time to root, to take hold.

You called it love.

That he had. Maybe it was, maybe it wasn't. All he knew was that he hadn't felt this happy, this content, in years. His work was his life and he was completely dedicated to it, but there was no denying that even when it took up every waking minute of his day, there was still an emptiness inside him that his work couldn't fill.

Not the way being with Bethany could.

It was lunchtime and he was hurrying to one of the small enclosures that was laughingly referred to as an office. Currently, it was Bethany's office. He was going to surprise her by stopping in to see if she wanted to have lunch with him.

He knew it would catch her off guard because ordinarily, she was the one who swung by his office and extended the offer. She'd been doing it for the last few days. Days in which they saw each other every day, sometimes for just a few minutes, sometimes for longer.

And sometimes, especially lately, all through the night.

He was grateful for this, grateful for the lightness he felt inside because of it. Otherwise, he seriously doubted he would be equal to everything else that was going on.

Like most people, he could handle one or two problems, or even three. But somehow, of late, he felt as if everything was conspiring to band together and crush him. He *needed* what was happening between him and Bethany.

Her door was open. He might have thought that unusual but the heating was on the blink again and doors were open all along the floor in a desperate attempt to share warmth.

He had his own ideas about how to share warmth, he thought, smiling to himself.

About to knock despite the open door, Peter heard her voice. She was talking to someone. Because there were no audible responses and she still carried on a conversation, he assumed she was on the phone. Not wanting to interrupt her, he stood there and waited until she was finished.

Looking back later, he would have been better off if he'd gone ahead and knocked rather than waited outside her door—and listened against his will.

"No, no, don't worry," she assured whoever she was talking to on the other end of the line. "I've got the man practically eating out of the palm of my hand."

Peter straightened, alert now. He didn't believe in eavesdropping, but she was talking about him, he was certain of it. What other man could she be referring to? Her tone unnerved him. Was she just amusing herself at his expense?

"Right," she was saying. "Yes, yes, when the time comes, he'll see things my way. I'm good at this kind of thing, don't worry," she repeated. "I can persuade him one way or another."

Peter felt something inside his chest twist and freeze.

So that was it. That was why a beautiful woman was making all the first moves. She was playing him. Manipulating him so that "when the time comes" in her words, he'd be so taken with her, so completely mesmerized and captivated by her, he'd vote her way for the takeover instead of following his beliefs.

Damn, what was the matter with him? Hadn't his time with Lisa taught him anything? He should have realized that a woman as upscale and classy as Bethany Holloway wouldn't even notice someone like him unless there was a specific reason.

How could he have been so stupid? So willing to believe she felt things for him? No woman looked at him romantically.

He should have realized that Bethany wouldn't, either. What he'd mistaken for electricity between them was only the static variety, brought on by dry air, not full hearts.

What Bethany hadn't been able to do using logic, she was hoping to accomplish using her body.

Angry, he felt like confronting her, calling her out on this. But he wasn't the kind to shout, to air his feelings or grievances in any place remotely public.

Instead, he turned on his heel and walked away.

He was nearly at the end of the corridor, about to make a turn around the corner when he heard his name being called.

"Peter!"

Bethany had obviously emerged from her office, more than likely to come over to his. Although he stopped, he made no effort to turn around. He didn't trust himself to be civil quite yet. His anger wasn't fully harnessed yet.

He dug his nails into his palms, forming fists, his back to her. "Yes?"

"I was just coming to see you. Are you up for lunch?" she asked, her voice bright and cheery. The very same voice that had moments ago bragged about holding him in the palm of her hand.

He heard her closing her door, undoubtedly confident of what his answer was going to be. But he couldn't look at her right now. Couldn't sit across from her in the cafeteria or the small coffee shop down the block and pretend that nothing was wrong. Pretend that she hadn't just ripped his heart out of his chest. Within three minutes of their being together, there was no way she wouldn't figure out that he'd overheard her.

As Henry had pointed out, he was a lousy actor.

"No, I'm afraid not," he answered, his voice devoid of any emotion. "I'm busy." And with that, he picked up his pace and walked away as fast as he could without breaking into a run.

Bethany stood there, stunned as she watched his back disappear down the hall.

That wasn't like Peter. Even when he was swamped, he was polite and lately, he'd been making time for her even when he was drowning in work. He'd never just brushed her off, not even that first time in the cafeteria when she'd tried to argue him around to her point of view.

She was making too much of it, she told herself. The man wasn't a superman, he couldn't be upbeat *all* the time. Besides, he was still terribly concerned about NHC's push for a takeover. That, added to Peter's already full-to-the-bursting-point day, undoubtedly put a strain on his good humor.

Still, she couldn't help feeling he'd just abandoned her.

A small voice, sounding a great deal like her mother, whispered, *Told you it was too good to last.*

Clenching her fists at her sides, she blocked out the voice, blocked out what it was proposing. Because she couldn't bear to think about it.

With a sigh, Bethany turned back and unlocked her office door. She wasn't hungry anymore. Her appetite had evaporated.

* * *

He wasn't taking her calls.

It was two days later and every time she called Peter's office, his nurse said he was with a patient and too busy to come to the phone. The woman mechanically assured her he would call her back later.

But he never did.

Just as he wouldn't answer his cell phone whenever she called. Bethany damned call waiting for identifying her number to him, foiling any possibility of actually getting him to pick up and talk to her.

Why was he avoiding her?

Something had definitely changed and she didn't know why or what. She tried her best to sit tight, hoping that whatever it was would pass, that it had nothing to do with her but just the workload he was staggering beneath.

But the sinking feeling in her stomach as she watched Peter walk in for the board meeting at the end of the week told her she was wrong on both counts.

It had everything to do with her. Whatever "it" was.

When he crossed the threshold, the last to arrive, Peter didn't look her way. Instead of sitting beside her as he had done the other meetings, he chose one of the other two empty chairs, sitting down in the one that was farthest away from her.

That stung. Part of her wanted to ignore Peter, to show him that if he wanted to withdraw from her, that was fine with her. She didn't need him.

But the other half told her that she did. That since she'd been with him, she'd felt more self-confident, more alive. Happier. Being with Peter had made her feel like a complete woman.

A woman who, for some mysterious, whimsical reason, he'd decided to fling aside, ignore and be downright rude to.

Well, she damn well wasn't going to stand for it.

Bethany could feel herself fidgeting inside as Larry Simpson droned on, reading the minutes of the last meeting, a meeting that had been as exciting as watching paint dry the first time around. Listening to it rehashed for a second time was excruciatingly boring. Especially when all she wanted was for the meeting to be over so that she could confront Peter in person since she'd been unable to do it these past few days. Wherever she was, he was always somewhere else.

It was almost as if he were intentionally playing a game of hide-and-seek with her. A game she was in the process of losing.

She didn't like to lose. She liked feeling empty even less.

The meeting dragged on. Neither she, nor Peter she noted, had any of the food that Wallace had brought in. It was the chairman's way of trying to make up for the fact that the board meeting was taking place during their regular lunch hour.

Peter looked ready to flee at any second, she could tell by his body language. Whatever was being discussed wasn't even registering—not with her and not, she suspected, with him. She vaguely heard that Wallace said something about a J.D. Sumner arriving later today. Sumner, she gathered, was from NHC.

She saw the veins in Peter's neck stand out, but he said nothing.

And then Wallace dropped a bombshell. "And there might have to be an investigation to verify if these allegations of insurance fraud are indeed true."

"Insurance fraud?" Bethany echoed, startled.

Wallace looked a little perturbed, but whether it was with her for speaking out of turn or with the situation in general she had no way of knowing.

"Yes." Anger creased Wallace's normally cheerful face. "Apparently two or more of our doctors are suspected of some sort of wrongdoing. Nothing is clear yet, but this is obviously muddying the waters."

Peter scowled. She could almost hear the rumble of thunder as his eyes darkened.

"It's a set-up," he replied in a low, hard

voice. All eyes turned in his direction. "Engineered by NHC to get Walnut River to capitulate. They assume that we'd be eager to get out from under this about-to-break scandal and accept any offer they make." And Bethany saw him turn to look at her for the first time that morning. He aimed the words directly at her. "They couldn't be more wrong."

Chapter Fifteen

The second the meeting was over, Peter was up and out the door. Bethany followed suit, bolting from her chair and taking off after him.

"Bethany, a word," Wallace called to her.

"I'll be right back, Wallace," she promised as she hurried out the door. She had no intention of losing this opportunity to talk to Peter. If he was going to ostracize her for something, she was damn well going to find out what it was.

Drawing in her breath, she fell into step beside him, lengthening her stride considerably to stay abreast. She'd never realized precisely how long his legs were until this moment. "I have to talk to you."

He didn't bother sparing her a look. There was still a soft spot in his heart for her and he wasn't about to allow that to undermine his resolve. "Sorry, but I'm afraid I'm busy."

God, but he made her angry. "You've been *busy* a lot lately," she said sarcastically.

"Well, you know how it goes. Running an antiquated hospital like this takes up a good deal of time. For those of us living in the Dark Ages, it requires more effort than most expect."

His response, not to mention his somewhere-below-freezing tone, left her stunned and temporarily speechless. She almost stopped trying to keep up.

Maybe this was the real man and the other had been a fleeting illusion, someone who really didn't exist. Maybe instead of the saint that everyone claimed Peter Wilder to be, he was actually just a colossal, boorish, self-centered jerk.

But he'd been a kind and gentle lover, she reminded herself. Could a man who was thoughtful in bed *be* that much of a jerk out of it?

No, damn it, Bethany thought. She was tired of rationalizing, tired of trying to pretend this didn't hurt like hell and that all Peter needed was a little space so things would get back to where they'd been a few weeks ago.

No more making up excuses for him. She wanted answers and she wanted them *now*.

Determined, Bethany picked up her pace and hurried after him again.

She managed to catch up to Peter just as he got on the elevator—bound for the next saints convention for all she knew. She stuck her hand in between the shutting steel doors. They came in contact with her fingers, then bounced back.

Getting on, she glared at him. "I said I needed to talk to you."

If he was surprised by her relentless determination, he gave no indication. What he did, staring straight forward, was repeat his response. "And I said that I was busy."

"I don't care," she snapped back. That finally surprised him, she noted with triumph. "Your ears are free for the next few seconds."

Peter looked at her, his eyes cutting her off at the knees. "You're going to need a lot more than just a few seconds," he informed her.

Finally, he was opening up. It was about time. "Then there *is* something wrong."

He faced the doors again, infuriating her. "There's a great deal wrong."

The doors opened on the third floor and three people got on. Their presence abruptly cut the conversation short.

Bethany pressed her lips together. There was no point in dragging out their confrontation in front of strangers, although, if she was forced to, she was willing to go that route. The bottom line was if Peter was going to treat her as if she'd suddenly developed leprosy, she wanted to know why.

When the doors opened on the first floor, Peter got out. Bethany was beside him like a shot, muttering apologies as she elbowed her way past the other occupants on the elevator who were obviously bound for the basement and the cafeteria.

"Would you care to elaborate on that?" she demanded, picking up the thread of the conversation that had been dropped. She kept her voice as low as she could, given the amount of emotion that was throbbing in it. For most of her life, she'd lived with one form of personal rejection or another. Her parents, the students at school, even her sister. Being with Peter, making love with him physically *and* mentally, had turned all that around for her. She was damned if she was going to lose that without knowing why.

She shadowed him step for step until they came to the entrance to the emergency room.

Stopping just before the inner doors that led to the treatment area, Peter looked at her coldly and answered her request with a single word. It drove a spear right through her heart. "No."

And with that, he walked through the swinging double doors, leaving her standing, dumbfound and crushed, in the hallway.

Tears, created out of equal parts anger and hurt, sprang to her eyes. Drawing in a deep breath, struggling for control, she valiantly tried to suppress them, to make them go back. She was too old to hurt like this. Too old to stagger beneath the oppressive weight of rejection.

She'd endured that all through elementary school, through high school. She was supposed to have left it behind her, be her own person by now, content to live in semi-isolation because she'd convinced herself she didn't need anyone to complete her. And then he'd come into her life, lighting up the very sky, and she'd realized just how wrong she was.

Was that all she was going to have? All that she was entitled to? A few weeks of happiness and now she had to go back to her cave?

Well, she didn't want to. At the very least, she didn't want to without first finding out what had gone wrong.

Did it matter? she asked herself, turning away from the E.R. doors. It was clearly over. This had been merely a fling, something women her age had all the time. A fling. Brief and exciting. To be enjoyed and then forgotten about. If she'd had more of them, if she'd lived like a normal woman, this wouldn't have been such a big deal for her. It would have been merely business as usual.

No, damn it, she thought angrily, it *hadn't* been simply a fling, not for her. And not, from everything she'd gathered about the man, for Peter.

There was something between them, something strong. He'd made her into a different person, maybe a better person or maybe her real self, she didn't know. All she knew was that she didn't want that person to go away. She didn't want *him* to go away.

Bethany turned back and burst through the E.R.'s swinging doors, Bethany stopped the first nurse she saw. "Where's Dr. Wilder?"

"Ella?" the woman asked.

She'd forgotten there were two of them. "No, Peter. The chief of staff," she added for good measure.

The vague look on the woman's heart-shaped face didn't inspire confidence. "In his office, probably. He's not on today."

So he'd walked into the E.R. just to get away from her. For a second, her stomach sank. But then she rallied. She was going to get to the bottom of this if it killed her.

Muttering a thank-you, she turned on her heel and hurried back to the tower elevators.

You're not going to get away from me that easily, Peter Wilder, she vowed.

J.D. Sumner turned up his collar as he stepped outside Walnut River General's front entrance. The wind whipped around him, chilling him to the bone as it brought fresh snow flurries with it. It was late. The moon was hiding behind one of the clouds.

It was too dark for him. He was accustomed to the ever-present glow of the city, 24/7.

He'd put in what he felt was a full day, trying to get on the good side of the hospital staff. More than a full day, he thought wearily. It had been a tough, uphill battle.

He had his work cut out for him, that was for sure.

While the members of the board had all been basically polite, he could feel the waves of hostility just beneath the surface. Especially from Wilder, the son of the founder. He supposed the man felt he had a personal stake in all this and J.D. was, after all, he thought with an ironic smile, the enemy.

While he was used to that, he had to admit there were times, like now, when it was wearing. He preferred to think of himself as a representative of the future, not the enemy. It was the only way he could continue doing what he did. He was the one the conglomerate sent out to smooth the way for NHC's inevitable takeover.

He wished there was no resistance. Didn't these people realize this was progress? The way things were going to be from now on, not just here but everywhere? Big was in, little was out. No more mom-and-pop shops, be they grocery stores, video shops or hospitals. Corporations were going to run everything and, in the long run, that was a good thing.

Or so he told himself.

The wind continued blowing, stirring up gusts, swirling the snow. He turned his face to the side as he continued walking.

And that was when it happened.

One moment he was walking, albeit taking baby steps, toward his partially buried car, the next moment his feet were no longer on the ground. They were airborne and so, for a split second, was he.

Trying to break his fall with his gloved hands, J.D. came down hard when he landed. The jarring sensation traveled all the way up, rattling his teeth, hurting the top of his head. Pain shot through one of his legs. The one twisted beneath his body.

It wasn't the kind of pain that bruising brought. It was definitely sharper, more excruciating.

Something had twisted unnaturally as his full weight came down on it, despite his attempts to distribute it. Was his leg broken?

More pain shot through him as he tried, unsuccessfully, to get up.

He called for help. The wind whipped the sound of his voice away, sending it toward the near-empty lot.

God, but he hated this insignificant little town.

The door to Peter's outer office was locked. Determined, Bethany circled around to the side door, which led directly to his small, inner office. When she tried to turn the doorknob, she was rather surprised that it gave. Unlike the one in the hallway, this door was unlocked.

Did that mean he was expecting her, or just that he was being absentminded?

No, she reminded herself, she wasn't going to overanalyze this. Whenever she did that, she only got in her own way.

With a quick knock, she swung the door open. Peter was at his desk, making notes in a file and cross-referencing them onto the computer. Surprised to see her, he recovered nicely.

Bethany pushed the door shut behind her. "You weren't on duty in the E.R." It was an accusation, not a statement.

He shrugged and went back to looking at the top file. "Slipped my mind. I thought I was."

Crossing to his desk, she moved the file, silently demanding his undivided attention. "Lying doesn't become you."

She couldn't read the expression in his eyes when he looked up. "I could say the same thing about you—except that it does. You looked beautiful, lying."

His words completely floored her. She had no idea what he was talking about. "When did I lie?"

The laugh was short and without a drop of humor. "When didn't you?"

She wanted a clear, direct answer. "I'm not in the mood for riddles."

He leaned back in his chair, mainly to put distance between them. She was too close and he could feel himself responding despite his anger at being duped. "And I'm not in the mood for any of your elaborate charades. I guess that makes us even."

"No," she contradicted heatedly, "because only one of us knows what you're talking about and it sure as hell isn't me."

He looked away, toward the window. It killed him to do so when, despite everything, all he wanted was to take her in his arms and kiss her. What kind of a fool did that make him?

Bethany deliberately moved so that she

was in front of him again, giving him no choice but to look at her. She had a panicky certainty, growing disproportionately by the moment, that if she let this misunderstanding between them mushroom, she was going to lose the best chance she'd ever had at happiness.

She meant to do or say whatever it took to unscramble this mess. "Look, I'm new at this, at trying to correct whatever it is I did, or you think I did. Help me out here," she said, "because right now, I'm in the dark."

He almost believed her, almost believed that she meant what she said. But then, she was good. She'd bragged as much to whoever she'd been talking to the day he overheard her. "There's no point."

"There is *every* point," she insisted desperately. "You can't make me fall in love with you and then just walk off into the sunset like some John Wayne wannabe. Not without some kind of explanation." She was pleading now and she knew it. But she was in too deep to care about her pride.

Peter looked at her, completely stunned. "You're in love with me?"

"Yes," she snapped. She could feel tears forming again and it made her angry to be that helpless in the face of her emotions. This wasn't fair. She didn't want to cry in front of him. She was risking everything and he was just sitting there, unaffected, damn him. "And it's all your fault."

He shook his head. He'd never wanted to believe anyone so much in his life. But he'd heard what he heard, the unguarded truth, said when she thought no one was around to hear her.

"Are you that desperate to get me to vote for the takeover?" he asked.

For a second, she was speechless and dumbfounded. This was coming out of nowhere. "What in heaven's name are you talking about?"

He sighed. She was good, denying everything until the very end. "Don't play dumb, Bethany. It's not like you."

She squared her shoulders, the walking wounded refusing to succumb to her injuries and fall. "I've always been proud of my intelligence. It's all I had and I never thought I would *ever* say this, but I am not playing dumb. I *am* dumb, ignorant of whatever it is I was supposed to have done that set you off this way."

He was tired of going around in circles. If she wouldn't give him the courtesy of owning up to it, he was going to have to tell her. "I heard you."

"Probably the whole fourth floor has heard me," she acknowledged, lowering her voice. "I'm not accustomed to yelling."

The woman was incredible. She was going to go down fighting. If it wasn't that she'd skewered his heart, he could almost admire her grit. "No, I mean I heard you when you were on the phone on Monday."

He was ringing no bells. She shook her head, not following him.

It almost physically hurt to say the words. "You were telling whoever you were talking to that you had me in the palm of your hand. That you could get me to see things your way. *Now* do you remember?" he demanded. Frustrated, he got up, turning his back on her and looking out the window.

"I never—" And then it hit her. Like the proverbial ton of bricks. She understood everything. Her hands flew to her mouth, as if to contain the shock. "Oh my God."

He turned around. She looked as if she was in shock. He supposed losing didn't agree with her. Well, winning this time didn't agree with him. He would have given anything if he hadn't overheard her, if he could have just continued the way he was, ignorant of her real objective.

"Coming back to you now, is it?" he asked sarcastically.

"Yes, it's coming back to me." Incensed that he would think this of her, she fired straight from the hip. "I was talking to someone about taking over Henry's job. Since he's considering retiring in a couple of months, the person I was talking to has the right qualifications. I told him that if he applied and really wanted it, I could probably convince Henry to see things his way—my way," she amended, using the phrase he'd said he overheard. "Henry's a dear and we get along rather well."

The anger vanished so quickly it left him almost breathless. He felt like a fool. "*He's* the one you have in the palm of your hand?"

She shrugged. "It wasn't the nicest thing to say, but I had my reasons. I exaggerated because the person I want to hire tends to need a fire lit under him before he makes a move."

Someone she cared for? Someone who was less of an idiot than he was? "This person—"

Bethany could almost see the questions forming in his head. She was quick to get in front of them.

"—Is my cousin. Distant cousin," she emphasized. Now it was her turn to be indignant. "How can you possibly think that I'd try to manipulate you after you and I— after we've—" She was so overwhelmed she couldn't get herself to finish the sentence. "Don't you realize that I think you're the most honorable man I've ever met? That I think it's wonderful that you're willing to stick to your principles even when that's not the popular stance to take?"

She looked into his eyes, searching for a sign that he understood how she really felt. Searching for the man she'd fallen in love with.

"I wouldn't want to change you even if I could. I like the fact that you stand up to me. I like the fact that you're you." And since she was being honest, she added, "I *don't* like the fact that you can turn me inside out like this."

The smile inside of him had been growing from the moment he'd realized what a mistake he'd made in not trusting her. From the moment he'd realized he hadn't made a mistake falling for her.

It curved his lips now. "Are you going to stop talking anytime soon?"

She was out of breath anyway. "Yes." Her eyes narrowed. "Why?"

He put his hands on her waist. The moment he did, he realized just how much he'd missed touching her these past few awful, agonizing days.

"So that I can apologize for being an ass." He drew her closer. "I am sorry, Bethany. Sorry I didn't give you a chance to explain. It's just that you're not the only one who's being turned inside out here." It occurred to him that she still might not know how he felt about her. "And you're not the only one who's in love, either."

"I'm not?" she asked in a whisper.

"Not by a long shot." He framed her face in his hands. "I love you, Bethany." His eyes held hers. "So what are we going to do about it?"

She grinned. "I hear that make-up sex is really great."

He had something more in mind. A lot more. And he had a hunch that she did, too. "Is that all you want?"

She looked into his eyes. And saw everything. "You know it's not."

"Me, neither," he confessed sincerely. "Marry me, Bethany."

He took her breath away again. The proposal was unvarnished. And perfect. "Just like that?"

"No, not just like that." She loved him, he thought. She actually loved him. He might never stop smiling again. "I've been waiting for you to come into my life for forty years."

Now that she was here, she had no intentions of ever leaving. "You're not going to be able to get me out with a crowbar."

After his terrible mistake, he didn't want to assume anything. "Is that a yes?"

"That's a yes." She slipped her hands around his neck. "Now can we have make-up sex?"

Peter smiled and said, "You took the words right out of my head," before he lowered his mouth to hers.

* * * * *

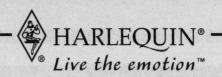

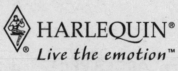

Harlequin® Historical
Historical Romantic Adventure!

*Imagine a time of chivalrous
knights and unconventional ladies,
roguish rakes and impetuous
heiresses, rugged cowboys
and spirited frontierswomen—
these rich and vivid tales will
capture your imagination!*

*Harlequin Historical . . .
they're too good to miss!*

HHDIR06

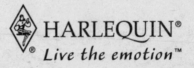

HARLEQUIN®
INTRIGUE®

BREATHTAKING ROMANTIC SUSPENSE

Shared dangers and passions lead to electrifying romance and heart-stopping suspense!

Every month, you'll meet six new heroes who are guaranteed to make your spine tingle and your pulse pound. With them you'll enter into the exciting world of Harlequin Intrigue— where your life is on the line and so is your heart!

THAT'S INTRIGUE—
ROMANTIC SUSPENSE
AT ITS BEST!

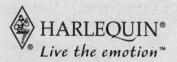

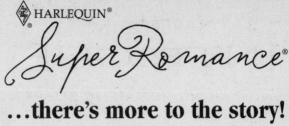
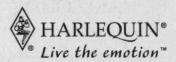